Welcome to Harlequin's great new series, created by some of our bestselling authors from Down Under:

THE AUSTRALIANS

Twelve tales of heated romance and adventure— guaranteed to turn your whole world upside down!

Travel to an Outback cattle station, experience the glamour of the Gold Coast or visit the bright lights of Sydney where you'll meet twelve engaging young women, all feisty and all about to face their biggest challenge yet...falling in love.

And it will take some very special women to tame our heroes! Strong, rugged, often infuriating and always irresistible, they're one hundred percent prime Australian male: hard to get close to...but even harder to forget!

The Wonder from Down Under:
where spirited women win the hearts of
Australia's most independent men.

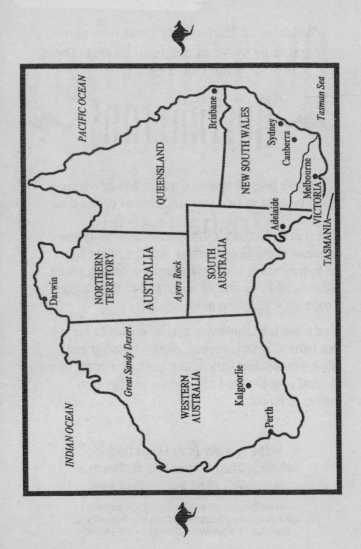

THE
AUSTRALIANS

BORROWED—
ONE BRIDE
Trisha David

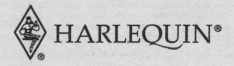

HARLEQUIN®

TORONTO • NEW YORK • LONDON
AMSTERDAM • PARIS • SYDNEY • HAMBURG
STOCKHOLM • ATHENS • TOKYO • MILAN • MADRID
PRAGUE • WARSAW • BUDAPEST • AUCKLAND

ISBN 0-373-82577-3

BORROWED—ONE BRIDE

First North American Publication 1998.

Copyright © 1997 by Trisha David.

This edition published by arrangement with Harlequin Books S.A.

Printed in U.S.A.

Most of **Trisha David**'s childhood was spent dreaming of romance far from the Australian farming community where she lived. After marrying a fabulous doctor, she decided doctors were so sexy she could write a medical romance and has since written a considerable number under the name Marion Lennox. Now her vision of romance has broadened to include romances for the Harlequin Romance® series, and she plans to continue writing as both Marion Lennox and Trisha David.

CHAPTER ONE

'HOLY cow, Beth, you should see the photographer. He looks just like a cowboy and he's drop-dead gorgeous!'

Fourteen-year-old Georgie Gallagher burst in the door—and stopped dead at the sight of Beth. The photographer was forgotten.

'Wow, Beth! You look fabulous!'

'Do I?' Beth's eyes moved to the mirror. Beth was stunned herself. This surely was a transformation.

Well, if Georgie thought she looked fabulous then she'd done her job properly. She was the bride Lyle wanted.

She certainly was! Beth's magnificent pure white designer dress showed her slim body to perfection. The lace bodice curved in to display Beth's tiny waist, then billowed out to a full circle skirt of satin. A soft net veil incompletely concealed her mass of red-brown curls, wide green eyes were luminous behind the netting, and clever flounces at Beth's breast hid the tiny leather pouch with ease.

Beth was now everything Lyle demanded and more. Her part of the bargain was fulfilled. The only trouble was...

'I feel so silly,' Beth confessed, stifling a smile at the sight of so much satin and lace. 'I look like a frilly doll. Good grief, Georgie...'

'You don't look silly,' Georgie declared stoutly. Then she grinned, teenage honesty surfacing. 'Well, maybe I do like you better in jeans, but Mum's even got me out of denim today.' The child crossed the room and gave her cousin a swift hug, and then stood back, troubled. 'Beth, I've missed you.'

'I've missed you too.'

'Not enough to visit.'

'No.' Beth hesitated. 'I can't afford to come to the city often, George.'

Georgie frowned. She crossed to the hotel window and stared out. The Manly ferry had just left the terminal and was moving slowly out past the Opera House, leaving a wide white trail across the smooth tranquillity of Sydney Harbour. Georgie appeared to find it fascinating. It at least gave her a reason not to look at Beth as she kept probing.

'Beth, Mum's always said you don't come home because you can't stand Hilda and Lyle. And Mum's right. Lyle might be our cousin but you know he's a creep. Why on earth are you marrying him if you feel like that?'

'Georgiana…'

'And don't "Georgiana" me.' The teenager scowled, still staring out of the window. She was clearly intensely troubled. 'Mum says you're old enough to know what you're doing, but heck, Beth… I don't understand. Is Lyle amazing in bed or something?'

'George!'

Georgie turned bright pink. She giggled self-consciously, then winced as her aunt's voice rose from the living area. Hilda was aunt to both girls—sister to Georgie's mother and to Beth's, before both Beth's parents had been killed in a car crash, but neither girl had any time at all for their not-so-maternal aunt.

'Bethany!' There was no ignoring Hilda's sonic boom.

'Ooh, yuk!' The teenager sighed. 'I'm s'posed to be giving you a message. Horrible Hilda sent me to say the photographer's waiting. He is too.' She leaned right out of the window to see the courtyard below. 'He's down there, and I must say, Beth, he's worth going down for. He came up to talk to Hilda and I almost reckon he's worth putting a dress on for. He's better than Lyle any day. Come on, Beth. Look!'

Beth hesitated, then shrugged. It wouldn't hurt her aunt to wait. Besides, Georgie was just learning to appreciate the male sex, and her comments made Beth laugh. If there was one thing Beth needed today it was laughter—and so Beth looked.

The photographer was bending over the luggage compartment of a sleek black Mercedes parked in the hotel courtyard. All Beth could see were legs—long, lean and really, really masculine...

The legs were clad in worn moleskin. Beth blinked. Moleskins, short-sleeved, open-necked workshirt and a wide Akubra hat. Georgie had described him as a cowboy and he certainly looked as if he'd come straight off a farm. He must be some photographer to get away with dressing as casually as this!

Who on earth was he?

It didn't matter. The wedding details had been left to Lyle and his mother. The man would be the best photographer money could buy, Beth knew, but Beth had had nothing to do with the arrangements.

'George, we have to go.' Beth pulled back from the window, but Georgie's hand restrained her.

'No. Wait and see. Honest, Beth, he's really something! I just want you to watch him turn round.'

So Beth watched as the moleskin legs straightened and a torso rose to match the body.

And then, despite her preoccupation with her approaching wedding, Beth's attention was caught. This was hardly an average city photographer!

The man had a build like someone who pumped weights— but this man hadn't built his muscles in a sweaty gymnasium. He was older than most of Georgie's fancies, being somewhere in his early thirties, Beth guessed. His weathered face spoke of a life spent outdoors, and his muscled body hinted at hard physical activity.

Georgie was staring down, entranced, and Beth could definitely see the attraction. The man was blatantly good-looking. Deep brown, unkempt hair showed traces of bleaching from the harsh Australian sun and his eyes were creased from the same bright glare. His face was lean and strong and...and about as different from Lyle as could be! He smiled at someone out of range, and it was as much as Beth could do not to gasp. Georgie wasn't the only one who could be smitten.

'What a hunk!' Georgie said with relish, leaning out of the window so far Beth hooked a hand firmly in her neckline and pulled back. 'Beth, you have to agree...'

'And you have to be kidding.' Beth smiled, pulling herself together. 'I'll be a married lady in an hour—and you're expecting me to say some other man's a hunk?'

'Well, he's miles better than your creepy Lyle,' Georgie said bluntly. 'And marriage doesn't stop you looking. Mum says it doesn't matter where a married person gets their appetite—as long as they eat at home. At least, that's what she told me when I found a copy of *Playboy* in Dad's toolbox. It's not what she said to Dad, though.'

'Your Mum's terrific!' Beth grinned. 'My favourite aunt!'

'You've only got Mum and Hilda,' Georgie retorted. 'And that's a great choice! Mum's always said she wishes she'd been able to look after you when your own mum died. It must have been horrid living with Hilda and Lumpy Lyle...'

'George!'

'Oh, heck...' Georgie bit her lip. 'I s'pose you'll be living with Lyle for good now, and I can't think why.' Georgie took one last regretful look down, and then left the window, turning her attention fully to the bride. 'I just wish I knew why you were doing this, Beth. Mum says there must be reasons and we're not to ask—but you're not pregnant, are you?'

'Of course I'm not.' Beth laughed and gave her cousin a swift hug. 'Don't be a goose.'

Georgie stood back and her sharp eyes raked Beth, as if checking out the truth for herself. She seemed satisfied. Beth's waist was so slim there was hardly room for a growing child.

And then Georgie's searching eyes moved higher—and stilled.

Her eyes grew enormous.

'Beth…' she said cautiously.

'Yes?'

'The flounce on your dress,' Georgie whispered. 'It just… It just…'

'Just what?' Beth asked innocently, turning away to collect the small velvet bag she intended carrying.

'Your flounce just flounced,' Georgie said slowly. 'All by itself.' The teenager darted round so she was in front of Beth again, her eyes huge. 'Beth, you haven't…?'

'Haven't what?'

Georgie gave a whoop of delight. 'Oh, you have, too. Oh, Beth, you haven't changed a bit! You've a baby down there. What is it, Beth?'

Beth sighed. She might have known Georgie would guess. Georgie's parents and Horrible Hilda lived within a couple of blocks of each other. When Beth had left home at fifteen Georgie had still only been young, but she'd been Beth's adoring shadow up until then and she knew Beth well.

'It's a tiny possum,' Beth confessed. 'A ring tail. She was brought in two days ago after her mum was hit by a car. For the first few days she has the best chance of surviving if she's feeling body heat and movement, and I'm not quite game to leave her in a heated pouch yet. The girl looking after my animals won't carry her on her so I had to bring him.'

'But your dress…' Georgie was still enthralled. 'It hides it beautifully. You're lucky your dress has the flounce.'

'It didn't until last night,' Beth smiled. 'I acted the modest bride and told the dressmaker my dress was too revealing, so

she spent hours fixing it, poor lady. Don't you dare tell anyone, George.'

'But does Lyle know?' Georgie demanded, entranced. 'Does
Lyle know he's taking a baby possum on his honeymoon? Oh,
boy! He'll have a fit! And, Beth, what if your baby needs a
feed mid-ceremony? Do you tell us to talk among ourselves
while you fish down your cleavage and haul her out?'

'George!'

'You're nuts.' Her young cousin grinned, linking her arm
firmly through Beth's and leading her to the door. 'You're
absolutely nuts, Beth Lister. You always have been and I love
you for it. I just don't know how the heck you're going to
stay married to your horrible Lyle!'

It seemed all the world was waiting for the bride. All Beth's
family and Hilda's friends...

It was mostly Hilda's friends and Lyle's, Beth thought ruefully as she submitted herself to their collective scrutiny. And
there'd be many more than this at the church. Lyle wanted a
huge ceremony.

'I want the best,' he'd demanded. 'The best church and
reception. The best photographer. The best caterer. I want us
to hit the society pages. We'll marry in style, Bethany, or not
at all.'

'Not at all' sounded pretty good right at this minute, Beth
thought bleakly, but a bargain was a bargain and she'd given
Lyle her word.

'The photographer's waiting in the lobby!' Hilda snapped
as Beth emerged from her dressing room, and Beth could see
her aunt was keeping the worst of her temper in check. Hilda
had been horrified when Lyle had announced he was marrying
his cousin, and she'd hardly spoken to Beth during their short
engagement.

'The photographer's a replacement,' Hilda continued waspishly. 'I don't know what Lyle will say when he finds out. The photographer your cousin employed is ill, so *this man* has arrived…' Hilda said the two words 'this man' as if she found the replacement photographer some repugnant form of insect life. 'His name's Kelsey Hallam. I've never heard of him— and he's not even in a dinner suit!'

'They don't wear them these days,' Georgie piped up from behind Beth. 'Only ordinary suburban photographers wear suits to weddings. The arty ones wear anything they like—and this one looks great to me.' She met Hilda's eyes with childish defiance—and then took a hasty step behind her mother.

'Who asked you, Georgiana?' Hilda demanded, but Beth could see Georgie's words had had an impact. Even if Hilda didn't approve of Lyle's bride, like Lyle, Hilda wanted the best. She and her son wanted the biggest. The most. If Hilda's only son was marrying then he'd do it with class.

Hilda glanced at her watch. 'Well, the man wants to take you to the waterfront for photos, Beth, but you be fast,' she ordered. 'Church in thirty minutes and you're not to keep Lyle waiting. Do you want me to come with you?'

'No, thank you, Aunt,' Beth said submissively, and lifted her train. 'I can manage alone.'

She always had. What else was new?

What was new was that Beth was about to become a married lady. The photographer was waiting. Beth's wedding was waiting.

It wasn't really new. It was just a hiccup before life resumed again as normal.

Just twelve hours of this, Beth told herself firmly, searching for courage as she pinned a smile on her lips. Twelve hours of Lyle and his horrible wedding, and then I can go home. And home will be all mine.

As promised, the photographer was waiting in the lobby. Kelsey Hallam was lounging on a settee. He untangled his rangy body from a pile of cushions and greeted Beth with a lazy smile as she emerged from the lift.

'Bethany?'

The photographer strode across the lobby to meet her, extending his hand in greeting—and he was just as good looking at close quarters. Bethany found her hand clasped between long, strong fingers imparting reassurance with their warmth. This man must be used to dealing with nervous brides, she thought fleetingly, casting an uncertain look up into Kelsey Hallam's penetrating brown eyes.

And the eyes caught her.

Around them the hotel receptionists were twittering with interest, and passing hotel guests stopped to stare at the exquisite bride, but Beth's attention was riveted.

They looked at her, this man's eyes, with a gaze that was distinctly unnerving.

Was this part of his job? Were these photographer's eyes? The eyes asked all sorts of questions—questions Beth wasn't the least sure she wanted to answer. Georgie's comparison with a cowboy flitted back into her mind, and she replaced it in her mind with another comparison. Bushranger? There was something about this man that seemed...that seemed almost dangerous.

'I'm Kell Hallam, and I'm very pleased to meet you, Beth.' The man was smiling down at her, using the same heartstopping smile that had smitten Georgie from a distance. 'Are you ready to catch the moment with some photographs?'

'Y-yes.' Somehow Beth managed to return his smile, though she knew her voice faltered.

'No bridesmaids?'

'No.'

'Well, that makes my job a whole heap easier.' He smiled, and nodded towards the black Mercedes parked out in the courtyard. 'I'll take you down to the harbour, if that's okay, Beth. Your fiancé demands the best, and specialised site work with natural backdrops is my trademark. We'll be back here in time for you to re-do your make-up before church.'

Beth faltered, and tried hard to stop her hand coming up to the pouch at her breast. It wasn't the tiny possum that was wanting reassurance now, she thought. It was Bethany Lister.

Photographs... It was all starting to sound so final. Still, a deal was a deal. There was nowhere to go but forward.

'Okay,' she said.

And in two minutes the photographer had Beth Lister where he wanted her. Kell Hallam had Beth in the rear seat of his Mercedes, driving in the opposite direction from Beth Lister's wedding.

The harbour was only five minutes drive from the hotel.

Kell Hallam manoeuvred his car past the long line of cars outside the hotel and then turned towards the harbour. His eyes smiled at Beth in the rear-vision mirror.

'Okay back there?'

'I just feel so silly,' Beth muttered as she adjusted the folds of satin and lace around her. Sitting in bridal splendour in the back of a photographer's car wasn't an entirely restful experience, and Kell Hallam's smile didn't reassure her in the least. It made her feel like jumping out and running!

'You need bridesmaids to keep you company.' Kell said, and smiled. 'I wouldn't worry, though, Bethany. You sure don't look silly.'

His eyes glanced at her again, and his look told Beth this man wasn't passing some empty compliment. The warmth in the photographer's eyes was enough to make her blush.

Good grief!

Beth looked fiercely down at her wristwatch, fighting down

colour. She was being as foolish as Georgie, she told herself. Beth Lister didn't react to men like this!

Her head could say anything it liked, but the colour in Beth's cheeks refused to agree with her. She stayed bright pink. How on earth to stay calm? Beth concentrated fiercely on her watch. Thirty minutes until she was married...

'We'll be fast, Beth,' Kell promised, seeing her raise her wrist and mistaking entirely the reason for her discomfort. He hesitated. 'Would you have been more comfortable if I'd asked your aunt to come with us?'

'No!' The rebuttal came fast and hard, and Beth winced as she heard the anger in her reply. She bit her lip, wishing the word back.

For a moment she'd allowed her feelings to show. There was no room for feelings today, she told herself harshly. There was no room today for what she felt for Hilda—or for Lyle.

'You don't get on with your aunt?' the photographer probed.

'Not much.'

'But she's to be your mother-in-law.' Kell Hallam smiled his heartstopping smile, robbing his words of impertinence with his rueful expression. 'Does that mean we have a nightmare of a marital triangle coming up?'

It would if this wedding were real, Beth thought grimly, imagining Hilda as a mother-in-law proper. Heaven help Beth if that *were* the case.

She managed to smile and shake her head. 'We'll work things out.'

'I'm sure you will.' They'd stopped at a red light and Kell Hallam lifted his eyebrows at her in the mirror, almost as if he knew she wasn't speaking the truth. His eyes gently quizzed—and in the end Beth had to look away.

She couldn't meet this man's look through the mirror. He

was too darned unsettling by half, she decided, stirring uncomfortably. He saw too much.

'You and the bridegroom are cousins, then?' the photographer asked cheerfully as the light changed and they started moving again.

'Right.'

'I guess this takes the description ''kissing cousins'' to extremes.' He smiled. 'Have you and your Lyle always been close?'

He had to be kidding!

'Yes.' For the life of her a fast affirmative was all Beth could think of to give.

'Your aunt seems in charge of proceedings today?' the photographer probed. 'Don't your own parents approve of the wedding?'

'My parents are dead,' Beth said with difficulty. 'I came to live with my aunt and Lyle when I was a child…until I left school…'

'But you don't live with them now?'

'No.'

This was no more than polite conversation between bride and photographer—intended by the photographer only to put Beth at her ease. Why, then, did she feel she was being put through an inquisition?

'So where do you live?' the photographer asked.

'I guess with Lyle, when we're married,' Beth said cautiously. The feeling she was alone in a minefield was becoming overwhelming.

'You won't both set up with your mother-in-law, then?'

'No!' Dreadful thought. Almost as bad as being married to Lyle.

'Figures,' Kell said thoughtfully. 'She's a strong lady.'

'Yes.'

One-syllable answers. They were the safest, Beth decided. This man's eyes were piercing and far-seeing.

Beth placed her hand surreptitiously on the pouch at her breast, but the tiny possum seemed to be sleeping. Long may she sleep, she prayed. If any man could pick up flounces flouncing all on their own, this man could.

The silence seemed almost ominous. Beth glanced at the back of Kell Hallam's head. There was a kind of watchfulness about him. A waiting... Once again, the word 'dangerous' sprang to mind.

She was being silly. Pre-wedding nerves!

'This seems a lot of trouble to go to for photographs,' Beth managed finally, striving somehow for normal conversation as the car continued its short journey.

Kell smiled and shook his head. 'Make the most of it, Beth. This is your day. You only have one chance at wedding photographs.' He hesitated and his eyebrows raised again. 'That is if you're planning this marriage to be for keeps.'

Once again there was that slight, almost imagined mockery, and Beth's fading complexion flushed all over again to an even deeper shade of crimson.

She *was* imagining things. Kell Hallam's face was openly pleasant. Surely he was smiling at her without a trace of mockery now?

How could this man guess what Beth and Lyle intended? Beth demanded of herself. He couldn't, of course. She was being ridiculous.

'What sort of photographs do you intend taking?' she asked.

'Boat pictures,' he said promptly.

'Boat...'

'A friend lets me use his yacht for my weddings,' Kell Hallam told her. 'It's a great setting.' Then, as he saw her eyes widen in alarm, he laughed. 'Hey, we don't cast off from shore. I'm a landlubber, lady.'

'Couldn't we just take a couple of snaps on the jetty and be done with it?' Beth asked nervously.

'But I'm an artist,' Kell growled. He grinned, as though enjoying her nervousness. 'And I have a temperament to match. You want me to show you my artistic temperament? Just suggest I take happy snappies instead of proper portraits!'

Beth managed a smile in return. 'I'm sorry.'

'So I should hope.' He smiled. 'I just hope you're sorry enough to be good and try to be photogenic for the nice man with the camera.'

'I'll try.' Beth's nervousness faded. Kell Hallam's laughter was infectious. 'You really want me to climb onto an actual boat?'

'If you want to avoid a tantrum,' the photographer told her firmly, his eyes still mocking with gentle laughter. 'I want to photograph you on the bow of the yacht, gazing seaward with longing. I want an expression on your face that says your beloved Lyle is somewhere out on the fearsome briny, braving dire peril to reach his bride.'

Beth couldn't help it. She choked on a chuckle.

'My "beloved Lyle" is the landlubber to beat all landlubbers,' she admitted. 'If he goes anywhere near the "fearsome briny" he'll be reaching for a bucket rather than his bride.'

Kell Hallam's answering chuckle lit his entire face. Beth could see his laughter-filled eyes clearly in the driver's mirror—and they held her in thrall.

She was worse than Georgie! This was a crazy teenager reaction to an attractive man. With a huge effort Beth made herself look away again.

'You're just what I need—I don't think!' The photographer was groaning through laughter. 'A pragmatic bride.' Then he turned firmly from the mirror to face the road. They were just turning out of the sidestreets onto the road down to the harbour.

'Enough,' he ordered. 'Look, lady, you let me get on with driving while you concentrate on a spot of romantic mood-setting. Get your face right—and it won't be right if you're thinking seasick and buckets. Think of romantic movies or Lyle in satin pyjamas. Close your eyes until we get there—and when we arrive I want you so in love I can't see you for love's sweet mist!'

Beth concentrated hard and found smiling was easy. Easy when this man had her in a delicious bubble of laughter.

Love's sweet mist was harder to come by. It certainly didn't materialise when she thought of Lyle—with or without satin pyjamas.

The little possum at her breast slept on, his warmth against her a comfort in itself. Beth closed her eyes obediently and tried to think romance, but nothing happened. Only the laughter remained—and the thought of Kell Hallam's dancing eyes.

Finally, giving it up as a bad job, Beth flicked her eyes open. They should be just about there.

They weren't.

They were still driving fast, but instead of turning down to the harbour they'd turned up onto the harbour bridge. Why on earth…? The road down to the harbour was clearly signposted. Why on earth had Kell missed it?

'Excuse me, but you've missed the turn,' Beth said, startled but not yet alarmed. 'We should have turned off before the bridge. If your friend's yacht's anchored on the other side of the harbour we'll never get back in time.'

There was a dull thud at Beth's side. Beth glanced across, just in time to see the lock on her door slide down.

The central locking system had been activated.

Her eyes flew to the driving mirror—and found every trace of laughter had faded absolutely from Kell Hallam's face.

'I guess it's time I told you that being late's the aim, here,' the photographer said, and his voice was one Beth hardly recognised. The laughter had completely gone from his voice. 'To make you late. Two weeks late, in fact. And it seems a waste to take wedding photos when there isn't going to be a wedding!'

For a moment Beth was too stunned to react.

What did this man think he was doing?

Beth stared at the mirror as if she hadn't heard right, but Kell Hallam was no longer looking at her reflection. The photographer's smile was gone without trace. The man's face was grim and set and he was concentrating only on steering the car in the fast-moving line of traffic out of town.

'What...what do you mean?' Beth stammered. 'I don't...'

'You don't understand?' Kell said grimly. 'Well, that makes two of us.'

Silence.

He wasn't going to break the silence either. A mile flashed past and then another while the shock settled heavily over her. For some crazy reason Beth couldn't begin to understand this man was taking her against her will.

Where?

Heaven knew.

Beth tried to make her stunned mind think, but she couldn't think past the locked door of the car.

Even if Beth could open the car door there was no way she could jump. The car was travelling fast on Saturday afternoon's quiet roads, and she wasn't crazy.

Crazy...

'What don't you understand?' she said at last into the silence, and her voice was a breathless whisper. Fear was starting to trickle in. She didn't know what was going on. All she knew was that she was in a fast car with a man who was clearly unhinged.

'I don't understand how Lyle Mayberry found himself a bride and organised a wedding in four short weeks,' the photographer said grimly. 'So I thought I'd come and fetch you and ask you to explain.'

'Explain what?'

'Why you're marrying Mayberry.'

Beth stared, her mind too numb with shock to think clearly. 'But I don't have to explain…'

'No?'

'No!' Beth took a deep breath, fighting fear. 'Let me out.'

'We're driving too fast,' Kell said calmly, but there was a note of steel in his voice. 'You'd hurt yourself and I don't want to hurt you.'

'Well, stop the car, then!' Beth was well and truly frightened now. There was just enough ruthlessness in Kell Hallam's voice for her to realise that whatever purpose he intended he was more than capable of carrying it out.

'No.'

Beth's heart was pounding double-fast. Unconsciously her hand stole up to cup the pouch at her breast.

'Why not?' she asked starkly, and Kell Hallam must have heard the terror. It was all around her, overwhelming. Beth could smell it…could taste it…

'I won't hurt you,' he said roughly, his eyes flicking from the road to her face and back again. They were travelling fast, north from the town towards the coast road. The freeway was Saturday afternoon quiet too, and the powerful Mercedes was going so fast he had to concentrate on his driving. 'You can believe that.'

'But why?' It was almost impossible for Beth to get her voice to work. 'Why should I?'

'Because hurting you is not in my plan.'

The veil round Beth's face seemed suddenly claustrophobic. She hauled it aside, letting her shoulder-length curls cascade unhindered.

'Your plan?'

'I'm not crazy, Beth,' Kell Hallam told her harshly. 'Angry, yes, but not crazy.'

'It's crazy to abduct me. It's crazy for a photographer to kidnap the bride he's photographing.'

'But I'm not a photographer, Beth,' Kell Hallam said, and his voice was suddenly almost gentle.

'You're not...'

'I'm a farmer, born and bred,' he told her. 'The fancy equipment is borrowed for the occasion. I wouldn't know one end of these complicated cameras from another.'

'But...please, I don't understand...' The man's voice was so darned reasonable. So sane! Fear was flickering through and through her, but it was hard to stay terrified when his voice was so calm.

'What don't you understand?' he asked.

Beth closed her eyes, fighting back an almost crazy impulse to laugh. She was very close to hysteria.

'Why are you kidnapping me?'

'I'm not kidnapping you,' he said evenly. 'I'm just borrowing you. Consider yourself on loan. Borrowed—one bride. To be returned, undamaged, in two weeks' time!'

'Two weeks?'

'Two weeks,' he repeated. 'The day after your cousin Lyle's thirtieth birthday.'

Lyle's thirtieth birthday.

The air went from Beth's lungs in a rush. Lyle's thirtieth. Somewhere in this crazy kaleidoscope of terror there was a grain of reason.

'You're trying to stop Lyle's inheritance,' she said slowly, her mind lurching into motion through the fear.

'Got it in one, lady,' Kell said roughly. 'You do know, then? I'm right, aren't I? You're not the misty-eyed bride Mayberry's been prattling on about.'

'I don't...'

'Mayberry's told the world he's been engaged to his cousin for twelve months,' Kell Hallam said harshly. 'But I've made enquiries. The first time anyone heard about this wedding was four weeks ago. So…are you in on the take too?'

'I beg your pardon?'

'Are you intending to play happy families with Lyle's fortune for keeps—or is Mayberry paying you a percentage?'

Beth's face froze.

'How…how do you know about this?' she stammered.

'Answer my question.'

'No,' she snapped. 'Why should I? Who and why I marry is none of your business.'

'Well, you're wrong there,' Kell said grimly. 'In two weeks I won't give a damn who you marry. But any woman marrying Lyle Mayberry in the next two weeks is very much my business. And, seeing it takes four weeks to get a license to marry in this country, unless Mayberry's had the foresight to provide himself with a back-up bride, then you're his only choice. So… For the next two weeks you'll be stuck nice and close to me. And then at the end of two weeks you and your precious fiancé can go to the devil for all I care. In fact, I hope you do!'

CHAPTER TWO

THEY didn't speak again for almost two hours.

For most of that time Beth stared straight in front of her, unmoving. Her mind jumped from one disconnected thought to another and fear overrode everything.

Kell Hallam took the car out through the Sydney suburbs and then north along the coast before turning inland through the Blue Mountains, up into Hawkesbury country, where the land was criss-crossed with waterways, wild and beautiful and remote...

After so long driving, Beth was starting to feel sick with the certain knowledge that Lyle Mayberry had lied to her, and that her cousin's lies had put her into peril. So much for Lyle's promises...

'This hurts no one, Beth,' Lyle had promised her. 'No one cares. If I don't inherit then the money goes to the public trustee to be distributed to distant relatives who don't even know the old man existed. The cost of finding them alone will probably take half the estate. Believe me, Beth. No one cares.'

Someone did.

Kell Hallam did.

Beth sat in the back seat of the luxury car feeling smaller and more frightened than she'd ever felt in her life—and only a growing wave of anger in the back of her mind kept her from bursting into tears.

Lyle had manipulated her—and now here was another overbearing male manipulating her for his own ends.

For money.

Finally it was Beth's little possum that made her break her

silence. She felt her wake and squirm, and then squirm some more, looking for the teat his mother would have had within the pouch.

This little possum's teat lay within Beth's velvet bag, hanging from her arm. Surreptitiously Beth removed the small bottle from her bag and cupped it in her hands, warming it gradually to skin temperature. She wanted a microwave, but the luxury Mercedes didn't quite stretch to that.

With the bottle warmed, Beth hesitated. She cast another cautious glance at Kell Hallam and slipped the bottle down her breast within the pouch to keep it warm. All she had to do now was lift the creature from the pouch and feed it.

And Kell Hallam would see.

He wasn't looking at her. He couldn't see her hands from his driver's position but he was aware enough of her movements all the same, and to feed a baby possum in the car without him sensing what she was doing was impossible.

He couldn't object—could he?

Lyle would have.

Beth knew all too well what Lyle's reaction would have been if he'd caught her with one of her babies. He'd done it once—when Beth had been about twelve—and the result still made Beth want to weep.

So… Was this man different?

Kell Hallam had laughing eyes and Lyle didn't.

Kell Hallam was ruthless.

He'd said he wouldn't hurt her—but Beth only half believed his promise, and to trust a defenceless animal to his kindness would be worse than criminal. She couldn't do it.

'Please…' she said in a small voice. 'I need to stop. I need to go to the bathroom.'

'Wait.' Kell Hallam's voice was harsh. Cold. Immovable.

'I can't wait,' Beth said stubbornly. 'I've waited for too long already. You have to stop.'

'I'm not stopping,' he said roughly, but to Beth's surprise the car slowed, veered from the centre of the road and finally turned onto a side road leading up into the hills. 'We're ten minutes from home.'

'From your home?'

'From my home.' Once again Kell Hallam's eyes met hers in the rear-vision mirror, and what he saw made him swear. 'I told you,' he said harshly. 'I won't hurt you. There's no need to look like that.'

'No need to be frightened?' Beth managed breathlessly. 'When you abduct me and cart me off into the mountains against my will? When I should be getting married right now and no one knows where I am? No need to be frightened…'

'Just shut up, Beth,' he told her. 'Believe me, I hate this more than you do. If I wasn't desperate…'

'Desperate for Oliver Bromley's money?'

His eyes narrowed. 'What do you know about Oliver Bromley?' he demanded.

Beth took a deep breath. 'Only that he died last month and left his home to my cousin.'

'His home and all his possessions.' Kell Hallam's voice was edged with contempt. 'And his fortune. He left them to your precious cousin—who looked after his affairs for the last few months of his life and so ingratiated himself with the old man that he left everything to him. Heaven knows whether the old man even knew what he was signing—but your precious Lyle made the legacy watertight. Or nearly watertight. The fact that after all his efforts he still had to find a tame bride must have made him really angry.'

It had. Beth thought back to the day four weeks ago when Lyle had come to see her. She hadn't seen Lyle for years, but Aunt Hilda had no doubt kept her son informed. He certainly knew her affairs.

'I know we haven't seen eye to eye in the past,' Lyle had

told her. 'But I know your lease expires on this place soon, Beth. I know you can't afford to renew it, and I'm in a position to help you.'

Lyle…help her? Beth had almost laughed aloud—and it had only been when Lyle outlined how much he needed her that she had been able to see that he might.

Oliver Bromley had left Lyle a fortune, but the fortune was provisional on Lyle being married. If Lyle wasn't married then everything would revert to the public trustee. If Beth agreed to marry him then Lyle would hand her the title of her precious farm as a wedding gift. They needn't stay together and in twelve months would divorce.

As simple as that.

Beth's heart had screamed at her not to do it—but the alternative was horrible. To lose her farm… To lose the only place where she'd ever been needed—where she'd ever been happy…

She had finally agreed, on condition that it hurt absolutely no one.

'No one could possibly even mind,' Lyle had assured her over and over.

Well, Kell Hallam was definitely someone. Another schemer. A man intent on abduction. A man outside the law.

Beth had thought of him fleetingly as a bushranger. The description was apt, and it scared Beth to death. If she was in this man's way…

Beth looked out from the car as it slowed and turned towards an entrance set back among the gums a hundred yards from the road. A wooden sign set among the gums stated the property name—'Coolbunna'.

The car bumped over a cattle grid set at the start of a long driveway leading into deep bush, and Beth gazed around her with a sinking heart. There was nowhere here she could run. This was wild, beautiful country—rugged, mountainous and lushly green. The property had been well named—'coolbunna' was the Australian native name for mistletoe, and all among the gums were brilliant green mistletoe outgrowths with their distinctive bright red blooms. Mistletoe was sometimes a problem in bushland, but here it was of no concern. The forest was so rich and dense in the uncleared areas that the native mistletoe was no threat at all.

But the denseness of the bushland was a threat to Beth. The land past here was high cattle country and the farms were far apart. The last farmhouse they'd passed had been two miles back. Two miles. Could Beth run so far without being caught? Not on the road—and if she went into the bush…

'You'd never be found,' Kell said harshly, and Beth looked up to find him watching her. 'Don't get any stupid thoughts about running. Besides, I have dogs. I've trained them well and they'd track you within minutes.'

'I'm not staying here. I can't…' A new fear was surfacing now, and it had nothing to do with her personal safety. Two weeks… Two weeks of imprisonment… Caroline had promised to care for the animals for two days, but Beth had said she'd be back by Monday. At midday on Monday Caroline would leave, whether or not Beth was back.

'Please, I can't…' Beth's voice rose in urgency. 'Look…Mr Hallam…whatever your name is…I can't stay here. If there's really someone Lyle's hurting by inheriting then I won't marry him. I'll promise, if you like, but I must get back. I can't—' Her voice broke on a terrified sob and Kell Hallam swore.

'Save your tears, lady,' he said roughly. 'I made myself a vow and no amount of histrionics is going to alter that. For the next two weeks you'll be here, so get used to it.' And the car swung round a bend in the drive to reveal Beth's prison.

It was some prison.

The house had been built at the turn of the century—and on the grand scale. It was a homestead in every sense of the word. The house was whitewashed stone, long and low, with wide verandahs running the full length of the house, stone steps leading up through the garden and vast French windows opening the house up to the bushland around it. The house looked wonderful—and so did its setting.

The garden around them was breathtaking. Lush green lawns swept around the car in a gracious curve. The scent from the stands of native frangipani clustered in golden blooms around the garden permeated through the car as they drove. There were yellow and white and crimson roses in massed profusion—and wisteria and bougainvillea and...and so much—all of it carefully nurtured yet encouraged in its wildness, so one wasn't sure where garden ended and bushland began. The lawns ran down to the river below the house, a river wide and deep and free, and behind the house the Blue Mountains towered in the distance like massive guarding sentinels.

In another time Beth would have been entranced. As it was her breath drew in in fear, and as a pair of dogs launched themselves with joyous welcome at the approaching car her hand came up to her breast and she closed her eyes in terror. This was like some ancient magic keep, specially designed to hold prisoners in thrall with its wonder.

When Beth finally found the courage to open her eyes, the car had swung behind the house and was pulling into a cluster of garages and stables. There was no one in sight. Not a soul except the dogs.

Kell Hallam stopped the car and emerged, whistling the dogs to heel and greeting them with a careless stroke of his hand. The dogs wriggled in ecstatic delight. Hallam threw open the rear door and the dogs peered at Beth with avid interest. They started towards her but were called back with a curt command from their master and ordered to sit two yards from the car.

'You're to stay here until I fetch you,' Hallam ordered Beth roughly. 'If you move my dogs will attack. As long as you stay in the car then you're quite safe. I'll be ten minutes.' He gave a faint, rueful smile. 'Cross your legs until then, lady. In ten minutes you can spend all the time in the bathroom you want.'

And he was gone, striding out across the yard towards the house with the long, lazy stride of a farmer. Of a man of the land... And Beth was left with the dogs.

And one hungry possum.

She looked out at the dogs and they looked back at her. Kell Hallam had told her they'd attack.

For the first time since her abduction Beth found herself tempted to smile. The dogs were a very elderly kelpie, dust-red and bushy, with a tail which quivered with innate friend-liness, and a younger collie, black and white, sleek and glossy, eyes bright with intelligence—his tail also twitching with ea-gerness to make a new friend. Their master's order to stay kept both dogs rooted to the spot, but Beth knew enough of her power with animals to know she could make friends with these two in a flash.

She was almost tempted, just to spite Kell Hallam, but her possum was getting more and more agitated at her breast. Carefully she closed the car door against her two interested spectators, delved deep among the satin to retrieve her baby and settled back in the car to feed.

It was a weird and strangely calming hiatus—this break in time where Beth could sit in silence with the small wild crea-ture placidly cradled among the satin folds as it drank.

The silence seemed almost overwhelming. Here among the hills there was no sound of distant traffic. No hum of a gen-erator or an engine of any kind. It was a calm and windless day, and there was only the high sweet call of bellbirds in the gums around the house and the tiny contented sounds of Beth's little possum drinking magnified in the stillness. Outside the car the dogs settled in contented pleasure, as if they enjoyed their duty as guard.

After about five minutes there was the sound of a car being started round at the front of the house but Beth couldn't see it. She heard it drive off into the distance, leaving her again only with silence. For a moment she contemplated the possibility that Kell Hallam had simply left her here, under the guard of his two watchful companions.

No. He wouldn't be fool enough to do that. He'd know that these two gentle dogs could be easily tamed. He'd have to stay.

He'd threatened her with the dogs if she fled into the bush. The dogs were no real threat to her safety—but Beth knew they would find her if she went. They might not attack, but well trained dogs in this country could lead their master to a quarry as surely as any master tracker, and if Kell Hallam had a horse she could not escape him.

Of course Kell Hallam had a horse. There were stables beside the garages and she only had to look at the man to know he'd been raised on horseback. They had a look of it, the men of the bush. Outback men...

Bushrangers...

So there was nothing for Beth to do but finish feeding her baby, tuck it back down into its warm, safe pouch, clasp her hands to stop their trembling and wait... Wait for her fate.

Beth's abductor was true to his word.

He returned as promised, slightly after ten minutes, striding back towards her with the calmness of a man coming to collect baggage from the car. Something of no importance. He whistled the dogs to heel and the dogs welcomed him with joy.

He couldn't be all bad, Beth thought briefly—not with dogs

who adored him as these did. Animals were the best judges of character, she'd decided years ago, and some of her fear receded a little. Surely if he did love animals then she had a chance. She tilted her chin and met his look as he came towards her, her green eyes flashing defiance.

'Prepared the dungeon, then?' she asked, and there was only the faintest trace of a tremor in her voice to betray her fear.

'There's no dungeon,' he told her, the smile he'd used as he greeted the dogs fading from his eyes. 'You're a guest in my home for two weeks.'

'A guest against my will.'

'And a guest I'd rather not have,' he flung back at her. 'Your cousin's plans gave me no choice.' He flung open the car door to let her out, and then moved to the luggage compartment. To Beth's absolute astonishment a pair of rather shabby holdalls appeared. She recognised them instantly.

'How...?' She emerged from the car to stand in open-mouthed amazement. 'They're mine. How did you get them?'

'From the hotel,' he told her blandly. 'You wouldn't have left without your baggage, now, would you?'

Beth licked suddenly dry lips. This man was devious, and— Beth was starting to realise—deeply intelligent. What he'd done was no spur-of-the-moment action but the result of careful planning over time.

'But...how did you get them?' she asked again.

Kell Hallam set the holdalls on the ground and then stood back, his deep eyes watchful.

'Maybe it's time you learned that you haven't been abducted, lady,' he told her. 'If you're expecting a posse of police headed by your cousin to come blazing down the track, sirens blaring, then forget it. You've planned this stunt for weeks.'

'*I've* planned...'

'You've planned,' he told her. He shoved a hand in his shirt pocket and produced a folded slip of paper. 'I made a copy of the letter you sent your jilted bridegroom, in case you're interested. Would you like to read the letter he received just before he set off to church?'

Beth stared up at Kell Hallam's implacable face. She took the letter without a word, unfolded it and read.

Lyle,
Thank you for your offer of marriage, but I've been given a better offer to stay unmarried. You inherit Oliver Bromley's fortune if you marry. I've been paid to ensure you don't. Lyle, our deal was financial. Before trusting it, you should have ensured I wasn't open to bribery. Two can play games like yours, Lyle, so you should have known bet-ter than to trust me.

Beth read the curt note twice and then let her hand fall. She stood in the warm sunlight, shock running through her body as she imagined her cousin's face as he read this. Would he believe she was capable of writing such a note?

Of course he would. Everything Lyle did in life was dictated by money. If Beth had been offered more to jilt Lyle at the altar, then Lyle would believe in her actions absolutely.

That wasn't to say he'd forgive her. Beth thought of her cousin's anger as he read this note and she blanched. She stared up at Hallam, to find him watching her with thoughtful eyes.

'My…my aunt…' she faltered. 'I…'

'You left another note explaining all to your aunt,' Hallam told her apologetically. 'It wasn't quite as nasty as the one you left your fiancé, but it was blunt. Something about your cousin thinking you were a naive fool and wanting to show him you could make some decent money too. Do you want to read it?'

'No, I do not,' Beth gasped. 'How dare you? How *dare*

you? And how…?' She was shaking with a combination of rage and shock and her voice was hardly more than a whisper. 'How did you get my gear out of the hotel? How did you get rid of the photographer? How…?'

'Money,' Hallam told her, his voice almost gentle. 'You and your cousin should know that money can buy many things. I cancelled the photographer—told him he was no longer needed as we'd found someone better qualified. He was furious, but when I paid him his fee and told him he was being paid for not working he took his money and his umbrage straight to the bank. His anger at being insulted ensured he wouldn't contact your cousin to confirm his dismissal.

'Then I paid people at your aunt's and your cousin's hotels to deliver the notes,' he continued. 'I'd done my homework well, you see. With the amount of noise your cousin was making about the wedding it wasn't hard to discover your arrangements. And your belongings—well, I knew you'd pack before you left for church, so I simply asked the concierge to see your gear was packed into my car. He'd seen me talking to your aunt and he knew I was connected to your wedding—so no problems. I don't think your cousin will send the police after me—not when you've so clearly organised this jilt all by yourself!'

'You…you…' Words failed her. Beth stood speechless, her foundations shifting under her. She was feeling overwhelmingly helpless in the face of this man's overbearing organisation.

'Now he'll know someone else is offering you money,' Hallam continued. 'But he doesn't know that someone is me. And even if he does—there's nothing he can do, Miss Lister. You're my guest here for the next two weeks—so I suggest you just swallow your anger, take that look of frustrated fury out of your lovely eyes and enjoy your enforced holiday. There's nothing else for you to do.'

*   *   *

Nothing else...

Beth was so angry she felt close to exploding. She didn't speak again—she refused to give Kell Hallam that satisfaction. Instead she somehow forced herself to docilely follow him while he showed her the rooms he explained were for her use.

'These rooms are my housekeeper's apartment,' he explained to Beth, ushering her into a lovely little sitting room looking north over the river. There was a small kitchenette to one side, a bedroom and a bathroom beyond. 'You'll find food in the refrigerator so you can fend for yourself. I imagine you'd like to see as little of me as possible for the next two weeks, and the feeling's mutual.

'By the way, I should explain that the phones have been disconnected for the duration, I've stabled the horses elsewhere and the only keys to any motor vehicle on the property are kept in my pocket.' He hesitated—then touched Beth's pale cheek for a fleeting instant and frowned as she flinched.

'It's a rough deal, lady,' he said softly as Beth's hand came up to touch the cheek where his finger had rested. 'But you should have thought of this as a possibility before you messed with me and mine. Come through and find me if you need me for anything important—just look for the dogs and I won't be far away—but otherwise I expect you to leave us alone. Now, though...if I were you I'd get out of your bridal glory and turn yourself back into Cinderella. Midnight's come and gone and your prince is nothing but a lying, swindling cheat.'

And with one last, long look, Kell Hallam was gone, firmly closing the door behind him.

CHAPTER THREE

BETH walked through to the bedroom and closed the door, as if to put as much space as possible between herself and her abductor. She sank onto the queen-sized bed but hardly noticed its luxury. For a long time Beth stayed right where she was, unmoving. Her hands clenched and unclenched within her palms but that was the only sign of life she gave.

She didn't know what to do. For the life of her, Beth Lister didn't have one clue as to what her course of action should be.

Lyle... Her horrible cousin, Lyle. He'd got her into this mess, but sure as eggs he wouldn't get her out again.

She was still dressed as a bride.

The realisation hit Beth with a sickening jolt. She stared down at her dress with distaste, and in a moment the gown was a crumpled heap of satin on the floor. Soon she was back in her habitual worn jeans and T-shirt. She crossed to the bathroom, brushed her curls free of the hairspray the beautician had used and scrubbed her face till her skin hurt, removing every vestige of the unaccustomed make-up. Then she stood and stared at herself for a long time.

The small bulge of the possum's pouch at her breast was obvious now, without the concealment of her flounces, and it looked as though she had a third breast—but it didn't matter. The normal Beth *was* this girl—unadorned, barefoot and with no pretence at all.

She would have to face Kell Hallam again, and soon, but first... First she had to get her bearings. She had to regain her

composure and find some sort of dignity with which to face
him.

Beth crossed to the French windows looking out into the
garden, hesitated a moment and slipped out to the lawn beyond.

The garden was balm to the soul. Here there was peace.
Kell Hallam and his dogs were no doubt still in the house, for
there was no sign of them, and Beth was free to wander as
she pleased. And she did please, her bare toes enjoying the
luxury of the cool grass with the rich soil beneath. She had
been in the city for almost a week while organising her wedding. A week was far too long...

The possum was restless at her breast. Beth hesitated,
glanced up at the house and then swiftly concealed herself
behind the fuchsia bushes flowering along the drive. The two
dogs travelling as a pack must make some noise. In this stillness she'd hear them as they approached, giving her time to
conceal her little creature. It wouldn't hurt to release the small
possum to enjoy the grass as well. It would do them both good.

So Beth lay full-length on the grass, her body forming a
protective curve between bushes and lawn as she released her
baby to the outside world for just a short sweet while. The
sun was so warm—and Beth was so tired... She lay and let
her mind go absolutely still. There was nothing in the world
but Beth and her small charge...

A hand touched her head.

Beth jumped about a foot—and when she landed a child
was crouched beside her, silently watching.

The child must have moved like a ghost, Beth thought in
startled amazement. The little girl was no more than five or
six, yet she moved as if stealth were her usual mode of travel.
She squatted now beside Beth's shoulders, an elfin creature in
a shabby pinafore, with plaited braids of fine blonde hair clum-
sily tied and big brown eyes far too large for her tiny face.

The child's fingers reached out to touch Beth's hair, as if to see if this strange, sleepy lady was real.

Instinctively Beth had gathered the tiny possum to her breast almost before she was fully aware who the newcomer was. Now, as the sight of her small visitor reassured her, she once more let the little creature go. The possum crouched once again in the protective curve of Beth's body and nibbled daintily at a fuchsia leaf—far too young yet to have learned to fear.

The child was watching the possum with wonder, and she remained absolutely silent. It was strange for a child to be so still. There was a wariness about her that reminded Beth of the wild creatures she cared for—the older ones, who'd learned humans weren't to be trusted.

'Hello.' Beth smiled.

The child didn't respond. Her eyes were wide and fixed on the possum, as if she was afraid to breathe for fear the little creature would vanish.

Beth hesitated, watching child and possum. There was the same fragility about them both, and despite her fears and the trauma of the day Beth felt her heart stir in recognition of a child's need. Something was wrong here...

'This is the first time this baby's been out of his pouch since his mum was killed,' Beth said softly, watching the child's face. 'I'm caring for her until she's old enough to be released into the wild.'

Silence. The possum nibbled on, and the sun warmed the trio and created an illusion of absolute peace around them. Beth didn't speak again. She felt no need. The child seemed content just to watch and Beth was content to let her be. She had two wild creatures now...

And finally it was the child who broke the stillness.

'You'll...you'll let it go?' The little girl's voice was a

breathless whisper, as if speaking was strange to her and a huge effort.

'When she's ready,' Beth said gently, turning back to watch the delicate little possum. 'Possums aren't pets, you know. They're meant to live free.'

Like I am, Beth thought fleetingly. Beth had always known she wasn't meant to have a family. What had she been playing at to agree to marry Lyle? Even when she'd been so tempted that she'd finally agreed, at the back of her mind she had known nothing but trouble could come of it. And now here she was, unwilling prisoner of Kell Hallam. This child's father?

The child was silent again—restfully silent for one so small. Like Beth, she seemed entranced with the little possum. There was another long, long silence.

Beth lay back with her face on the soft grass and let the peace and warmth envelop her. The child was by her side— and something told Beth that the child needed silence and patience almost as much as any injured animal. There was the smell of fear about her—traces of terror. If Beth reached out to touch her, she had the feeling the child would run for her life.

Maybe Kell Hallam had warned the child of Beth. If so, what on earth had he told her? That Beth was some sort of witch?

There was nothing to do but watch—and wait.

Finally the child spoke again.

'What…what's the possum's name?' she whispered.

'I don't know,' Beth told her gravely, considering the possum with care and not looking at the child. She sensed instinctively that the less attention focused on this little one the better. 'I guess only other possums know what her real name is. Do you have a name we could call her while she's with me?'

The child pondered, her head to one side and a look of

serious concentration on her face. The look on her face told Beth she considered that this was a matter of grave importance.

'Is it a boy or a girl?'

'A girl.'

'Then we'll call her Petal,' the child announced. ''Cos that's what she's eating and it suits her.'

It did, too. Beth watched the delicate little creature eat some more. Then, as the possum let the last leaf fall and looked anxiously about, she scooped the baby up and popped the little creature back in her breast pouch.

'Petal's only a tiny baby,' Beth explained at the child's look of wonder. 'She's tired and she mustn't get cold.'

'She sleeps on your tummy?'

'That's her favourite place,' Beth explained. 'It keeps her warm and my heartbeat underneath her reminds her of her mum.'

The child lapsed into silence again, considering. Finally she took a deep breath, as if coming to a decision. 'Do you want to know my name?'

'If you'd like to tell me then I'd love to know,' Beth smiled. 'My name's Bethany. Beth for short.'

The child nodded gravely and pronounced judgement. 'Beth's a pretty name. It's not as pretty as Petal, but...but I like it. My name's Katie, but my...my mummy sometimes calls me Katie-bell.'

'I'm very pleased to meet you, Katie-bell.'

Maybe with another child Beth would have reached out to shake hands with adult condescension—but with Katie she did no such thing. The child still seemed on the brink of flight—as if the slightest movement could drive her to terror.

'Do you like my dress?' the child asked softly.

Beth checked out the child's pinafore—pretty enough, but very worn and at least a couple of sizes too small. This, though, was hardly the time for honesty—not when there was such anxious pride in the child's question.

'I like it very much.' Beth smiled. 'Is it your favourite?'

'My mummy gave it to me. She made it on a sewing machine and I watched her.' The little girl closed her eyes and then opened them, as if searching for courage. 'If the possum lies on your tummy and thinks she can remember her mummy, do you think…do you think I could?'

Beth blinked.

'Maybe,' she said cautiously. 'Do you want to remember your mummy?'

'Yes.' The child sat down next to Beth, then with fixed resolution, lay her small body against Beth. She looked up through the canopy of leaves above them and when she spoke again her voice was rigid with tension. 'Sometimes now I can't remember her properly,' she said desperately. 'I can't any more. I was sure I could, but now…now she's getting all fuzzy.'

Beth's heart turned over. What had happened in this little one's life? Questions weren't important now, though. There was only this fragile, desperate plea for comfort.

Beth's arm came round the small shoulders and she pulled her close. The child held rigid for one long, long moment— and then seemed to crumple against her. Her face nestled against the pouch at Beth's breast.

'There are two heartbeats here.' Beth spoke into the child's soft braids. 'Mine and Petal's. Listen and feel…and then see if you can remember when your mum held you like this. I'm sure she did. All the very best mums do—and I think your mummy must be the very best to have a little Katie-bell like you.'

'Do you think so?'

'I really think so,' Beth said softly. 'And she sewed your

pinafore. What a lovely mummy to do that for her little girl. Now hush and listen.'

And there was no sound for a very long time.

'Katie!'

Three hearts jolted in unison at the sound of a loud male voice echoing across the garden. Almost before the second syllable had sounded, Katie was on her feet and backing behind the bushes.

And then, before Beth could move, the child was gone.

Beth rose to see the child race across the lawn towards the house, pigtails flying. Kell Hallam was there, standing on the verandah to call. Beth watched the tiny child fly up towards him—but instead of going straight to him Katie veered as she approached and went right inside the front door.

The door slammed behind her—and Kell Hallam was left alone on the verandah, staring after her.

What on earth…? What sort of strange relationship was this?

Slowly the man on the verandah turned and looked in the direction from where Katie had come—and saw Beth.

The dogs saw Beth almost at the same time. They'd emerged from the house with their master and were at his heels on the verandah. Now they saw this interesting stranger on their territory and bounded down the stone steps and across the lawn to greet her. Beth's hand flew to the pouch at her breast and she stood still, waiting.

For an instant Kell Hallam hesitated, glanced inside, as if uncertain as to whether to follow Katie, and then followed his dogs down onto the lawn.

By the time he reached Beth, the dogs were wild with excitement. They were bounding all around her, and Beth knew the smell of the little possum was all over her. The dogs could

smell the baby possum and they knew just where it was—
under Beth's hand at her breast.

'Heel!'

Kell's voice snapped out a firm order. The dogs looked back
at him to check if he was serious—and then reluctantly fell in
behind him. Kell Hallam came on over the grass towards Beth,
his collie and his kelpie safely at heel.

'What the hell…?'

It was quite clear from the dogs' behaviour and the way
Beth was cradling the not so concealed pouch between her
breasts that she had something which interested the dogs ex-
cessively. Hallam's eyes narrowed as he grew nearer, and unconsciously Beth brought her second hand up in a protective
curve.

'What have you got there?'

Beth stood her ground. She felt small in the face of this
man's height and strength—small and insecure. Her bare toes
curled into the grass, as if by linking herself to the earth she
could gain strength. It only made her feel even more insecure.
She wanted boots on—boots with studs and a leather jacket
with a skull and cross bones on the back—and at least another
six inches of height.

'Show me what you're hiding,' Kell demanded, and Beth
flinched. Her eyes met his, though, unwavering.

'You said you didn't want anything to do with me for the
next two weeks,' she managed.

'I don't. But you'll show me what you're hiding, just the
same.'

'No.'

'Then I'll let my dogs…'

'You toad!' Beth backed away, her face losing every vestige
of colour. 'What do you think I'm hiding? A gun? If I was
then I wouldn't be here now. You have all the power and you
know it. And how dare you threaten me? Scare me? How dare

you abduct me?' She took a deep breath. 'And you might have written all the letters in the world, but how will you explain things when I get back and go to the police?' And then her face paled even further. 'If…oh, God…if you let me go…'

The thought hit her with the power of a sledgehammer. This man might have covered his tracks nicely to make everyone think she'd run of her own volition—but if he finally let her go then he'd be facing criminal charges. He was a criminal. A kidnapper. A man even his own daughter seemed afraid of…

'Beth, I've told you. I won't hurt you.'

Kell Hallam had seen the terror wash over Beth—and he'd seen the thought. Now he reached out to touch her, but Beth moved back as if his touch would burn.

'How do I know that?' she whispered. 'How do I know you're speaking the truth. I don't. I can't.'

'You can because I tell you.'

'Oh, y-yes?' Beth stammered. 'Like Lyle told me no one cared if he inherited Oliver Bromley's money. Like you told me you were a photographer. You and Lyle… Why would I ever trust either of you? You're nothing but a criminal, Kell Hallam. And Katie… Why on earth does your own daughter fear you? What did you do to her mother?'

There was absolute dead silence.

No one spoke. Even the dogs seemed to draw breath.

Beth stood firm, her body trembling and her face white as chalk, and she watched conflicting emotions run freely over Kell Hallam's face. First there was anger. Then shock. Then incredulity.

'What about Katie's mother?' he said at last.

'Why is Katie so frightened?' Beth demanded. 'And why isn't she allowed to see her mother?'

'How—?' Kell's voice broke. He took a deep, ragged breath. 'How do you know about her mother?'

'She told me she can't remember her,' Beth told him 'She told me she—'

'She *told* you?' There was no doubt which emotion took precedence now. Absolute sheer astonishment. Kell Hallam took two fast steps and gripped Beth's shoulders so hard he hurt, and his face was dark with anger. 'You're lying,' he snapped. 'Look, I don't know what troublemaking scheme this is…'

'Why on earth would I lie?'

Beth's whispered protest sank home. For a long moment Kell Hallam stood staring down at Beth's face—her slight body was raised from the ground with the strength in his hands—and then finally he let her go so her bare feet sank back to earth. Beth's breath came out in a rush.

'Katie's mute,' he said blankly. 'She doesn't speak. I know you're lying but I don't know what game you're playing at. And what the hell are you wearing under your T-shirt?'

It was almost a full minute before Beth could find the courage to answer him—before she could swallow her fear enough to speak. There was so much going on here that all she felt was confusion—and in fact by the time she did open her mouth again confusion was starting to replace terror.

She watched Kell Hallam's face and there was no threat there. Anger had been replaced by a confusion as great as Beth's.

'I have a possum,' she told him at last, and watched the confusion grow.

'A possum.' Kell Hallam shook his head, as if trying to clear a fog. 'A…'

'It's a baby ringtail,' Beth told him, her voice firming in the face of his uncertainty. 'Caring for orphaned wildlife is my job. It's what I do.'

'Your job.' The man was lost. He released her shoulders

completely and stood back, staring at her as if she had suddenly grown two heads. 'What job?'

'It's how I make my living,' Beth said patiently. 'I'm a conservation and wildlife carer. It's my job to take in injured and orphaned wildlife and care for them until they can be released into the wild.'

'I don't believe you.'

'I'm not asking you to believe me,' Beth said flatly. She shrugged. 'But it's the truth. It's the reason why you have to let me go.'

'I'm not letting you go.'

'Then you'll have twenty deaths on your hands,' Beth told him. 'I have someone looking after my animals until Monday. On Monday if I'm not back they'll be left to starve. You have to let me go—or let me phone someone to come in and take over. You must.'

'Show me the possum.' Kell Hallam's face was blank with astonishment—and the astonishment grew as Beth obliged by pulling the soft leather pouch from under her T-shirt and opening the neck wide enough for a small, enquiring face to peep out. Kell drew in a breath of sheer shock.

'You... Where on earth did you get that?'

'I told you. I'm a wildlife carer.' Beth tucked the possum back where it belonged—back where it was safe. She tilted her chin defiantly. The tiny possum was in her charge. She had to be brave, if only to defend her.

'You didn't bring the damn thing here in your baggage?'

'No,' Beth agreed patiently. 'I carried her in a pouch around my neck, just like she's being carried now.'

'But...' You could see the thought processes at work. Kell Hallam was thinking fast—and as she watched Beth could almost see the vision of her bridal outfit being conjured up before his eyes to be inspected. And what he saw astonished him even further.

'You had it under your dress!'

'Got it in one,' Beth said dryly. 'Very good.' She took a deep breath. 'But, Mr Hallam...I only have enough milk formula with me to last this little one two days and I have animals at my farm depending on me. If I don't return then they'll die. You must let me go.'

Kell Hallam's face tightened. He stared at Beth as if he was trying to figure out just what sort of creature it was he'd got himself involved with—and by the look of what he was discovering he was none too pleased.

'I'm not about to let you go for any possum,' he said at last. 'It's a nice story, but if you've just caught the thing...'

'You still think I'm lying?'

'Do you expect me to believe you had the creature under your wedding dress? That you were going to be married with a possum hanging round your neck? And what about afterwards?' he demanded. 'You and your precious cousin? You were planning to head off on honeymoon with a possum in tow? I know Lyle Mayberry, lady, and frankly I don't believe you. And what about these twenty other animals then?'

'There wasn't going to be a honeymoon,' Beth said steadily, still fighting for courage. 'I was marrying Lyle and then I was going home.'

Home.

Why did the word have such a hollow ring to it? As if home belonged to another world. She looked up into Kell Hallam's bleak, hard face and she felt her foundations shift. Nothing was the same any more. Nothing.

'So you and Mayberry really were marrying for the money?' Hallam said carefully, his face watchful. 'You were doing it just for the inheritance?'

'That's right.' Beth swallowed, and swallowed again. There was no way she could escape this man. There were things going on she didn't understand—but it was starting to be clear to her that her only chance lay in being absolutely honest. And in hoping this man had more decency—more integrity—than her cousin.

She looked up at him and something stirred deep within. Some basic instinct telling her maybe…just maybe it was worth a try.

'Can I explain?' she asked quietly, and Kell Hallam nodded, unmoving. He stood like judge and jury all in one, his arms folded, his bare arms strong and sinewy and his face hard and judgemental in the sunlight. Waiting…

'I have a farm…' Beth started nervously. She dug her toes into the grass and felt the soft earth give a little. 'Not like this. It's tiny and I don't own it. I lease it. I trained as a vet nurse after I left school and then worked like crazy till I could afford the lease. It's only twenty acres but it's a lovely little farm, and I breed goats for cashmere to pay the rent.'

'So?'

'So I also work as a wildlife carer,' Beth said desperately. 'It's all I ever wanted to do. All that means anything to me. People bring me orphaned and injured wildlife and I care for them. I treat all sorts of native animals. Koalas, wallabies and kangaroos, and wombats. At the moment I have a little sugar glider who's nearly ready for release. Birds, too. I care for them and then take them through an acclimatisation process until they're ready to be returned to the wild.'

'And what's this got to do with me?' Kell looked as if he was trying hard not to be interested—trying to remain cold. The harsh look on his face had eased a little, however, and Beth fought for courage to continue.

'I have trouble with fencing,' she said sadly. 'I thought it was good enough, but…six months ago a couple of wild dogs got in and mauled my goats. They killed all the mature animals I had ready for market. The goats I breed are prized for their coats and a good animal is worth five hundred dollars or more. They killed fifty animals before I woke and drove them off.'

'That must have made a substantial hole in your profits.' Hallam's words were a flat comment, and Beth nodded.

'It did more than that,' she said bleakly. 'It ruined me. It meant I couldn't afford to meet the lease payments for my farm. I'm paid a small fee to care for the animals but it's not enough to fund the farm. The death of my goats meant I'd have to move, and I can't afford another farm. Without a farm I can't rehabilitate my animals as they heal. I'd have to find new carers for my animals and resign from my position with the Conservation Foundation. It meant the end of everything I'd ever worked for.'

Silence.

'So then?' Kell said slowly.

'So then along came my cousin Lyle,' Beth told him. 'My aunt keeps tabs on me and she found out what had happened— how broke I was. I think she was rather pleased. She didn't like me making a success of my farming. Anyway, she told Lyle and he came to see me.

'I don't like Lyle. I never have. As a child I had to live with Lyle and my aunt after my parents were killed, but they...well, my aunt always treated me as a poor relation, and Lyle enjoyed making my life miserable. I stopped trusting Lyle a long time ago, but this time... This time he was offering me hope. He said Oliver Bromley had left him an inheritance on condition he was married by the time he was thirty— but Lyle didn't want a wife. I can believe that. He's not into sharing, my cousin Lyle.'

'So what did he offer you?'

Beth hung her head and watched her toes in the grass. The bottoms of her jeans were frayed with age, and a thread was hanging across the bare skin of her left foot. She flicked it aside and then tried to pull it free with her toes. 'Thirty thousand dollars,' she whispered. The task of thread-pulling seemed to take her entire concentration. It stopped her having to look at Kell Hallam. 'The price of the mortgage on my farm,' she told him.

Silence.

Did he believe her?

'Beth, how much do you think Oliver Bromley left your cousin?' Kell asked at last, in a voice that was curiously detached. 'Did Mayberry tell you what his inheritance was worth?'

'No. But I expect…I imagine it'd have to be a hundred thousand or more to make it worth Lyle's decision to marry. He said he'd cover the legal costs of our divorce as well.'

'Generous of him.' Kell stepped forward then, put a hand under Beth's chin and pushed her face up to force her to meet his eyes. 'Bethany, your cousin stood to inherit more than a million dollars in cold, hard cash by marrying you. As well as that he'd inherit Bromley's home—worth a fortune in itself—Bromley's art collection and all Bromley's personal goods. Total value, well over two million. For that, the cost involved in a divorce settlement comes cheap—wouldn't you say?'

Beth's eyes widened. 'Two million…'

'That's what I said,' Kell told her harshly. 'If you'd done your homework…'

Beth shook her head. She pulled away from him and stared up through eyes that were over-bright with emotion.

'Do you think I care?' she told him fiercely. 'Do you think I give a toss just how much Lyle inherits? Lyle and his mother have been treating me like dirt since I was five years old. When I was old enough to legally live on my own I moved out, and if I never see him again I'll be happy.' She bit her lip. 'But now…I can see two million dollars makes a differ-

ence.' Her eyes hardened. 'Especially if it's you who inherits
if Lyle doesn't. I can see why you've gone to such effort...'

'No.' Kell's face firmed too. He shook his head. 'Beth, I
think...I guess we've both been guilty of misjudging each
other. I don't want any part of Oliver Bromley's money. He's
no relation of mine.'

'But...' Beth took a deep, ragged breath. Nothing was making sense here. She forced herself to meet his eyes, and her
chin tilted up in a token gesture of defiance. 'So why the
elaborate kidnapping? Why are you holding me a prisoner? If
you don't inherit Oliver Bromley's money when Lyle doesn't
marry—then who will?'

Kell Hallam met her look head-on, and his face softened.

'You really want to know?'

'Yes.'

'Then you can believe it or not, but it's someone who needs
it even more than you need your farm,' he told her gently.
'It's Katie.'

Katie...

Beth stood in the sunlight, aware suddenly that the heat of
the day was beginning to fade with the coming of evening.

Unexpectedly she shivered.

'Katie,' she said blankly. 'Your...your little girl?'

'Katie's not my daughter,' Kell told her. He glanced up at
the house. 'Beth, we need to talk, but I need to check Katie.
She's an independent child but I like knowing what she's
about. Will you come into the house?'

'Into your section of the house, you mean?' Beth demanded.
'Or the bit that's allocated as my prison?'

'Hell.' Kell Hallam put a hand up and ran it through his
thick crop of hair, leaving it ruffled and unkempt. His face,
for the first time, betrayed traces of the weariness and strain
Beth was feeling through and through.

'Beth, this is a bloody mess,' he said bluntly. 'But can we

at least get off to some sort of fresh start? You've been honest with me. It's time I was honest with you. Come inside and I'll check Katie and then make us both a drink. I could use one even if you couldn't.'

'I don't—'

'There's no choice,' he said flatly. 'Honesty or nothing.' And he took her arm and led her unresisting to the house.

CHAPTER FOUR

KATIE was in the house already and she was safe enough. There was a pile of children's construction blocks in a corner of the capacious farmhouse kitchen where Kell led Beth, and Katie was crouched over them. She stared up as the adults entered but didn't say a word.

What had Kell said? That the little girl was mute?

'Would you like a drink, Katie?' Kell asked, and the child said nothing. She simply sat staring at Kell while he produced lemonade from the refrigerator and poured a glassful. He handed the child the tumbler. She accepted it without a word and drank it with her eyes not leaving Kell's face—then bent over her blocks again. Communication ended.

The interlude left Beth feeling chilled to the bone.

'I'm having a beer,' Kell told Beth, his voice tense. He turned back to the refrigerator, as if to block out the child's indifference. 'There's wine, Beth, or...'

'I'd like lemonade as well,' Beth told him. 'If that's okay.'

'Sure.' He filled two glasses and then motioned to the back door. 'We'll sit on the verandah. I can watch Katie through the screen.'

Beth hesitated. She looked down at the little girl hunched over her blocks, hesitating as to whether to speak to her or not—but there was something about the child that prevented Beth from trying.

Keep away, the little girl's body language was saying, and Beth was wise enough to respect such a message. Nothing but trouble could come from ignoring it.

She took her lemonade from Kell and followed him out.

There were cane chairs scattered along the verandah, weathered from years of exposure but with deep, comfortable cushions that invited weary bodies to sink into their depths. Beth's body did just that. One dog sank beside her, the other flopped beside Kell, and they all turned their attention to the setting sun. This was a place of peace, but peace didn't sit easily. Each seemed deep in thought—even the dogs. Where on earth to begin?

It was Kell who finally broke the silence, and then it was a good ten minutes before he spoke. He'd finished his beer and the grapevines hanging down from the trellis along the verandah were throwing his face into deep shadow. Beth could hardly see. The tiny possum at her breast was fast asleep and she could feel her heart beating strongly through the leather of her pouch.

'Katie is my half-sister's child,' Kell said harshly. 'I guess that makes her almost my niece.'

Beth moistened dry lips and sought for the right words. The right words were impossible.

'But…she doesn't seem to know you very well,' she said slowly. 'You… She treats you as a stranger.'

'I am a stranger.' Kell sighed. 'My half-sister's de facto husband was Richard Bromley—Oliver Bromley's son—but I never knew Richard. Christine met Richard in America and never came home with him to Australia. I gather there was friction between Richard and his father—in fact father and son were an impossible pair, and Christine wedged herself firmly in the midst of them.'

'But…she loved Richard?'

'Who knows?' Kell said heavily. 'After my mother died, Christine cut herself off from her family completely. I hadn't heard from her for years until I was contacted on Oliver Bromley's death. It seems…well, I gather Katie was born six years ago and Christine and Richard carted her around the world in increasingly desperate circumstances. Finally—well, I don't know what the full story was and I don't want to—finally both Christine and Richard were killed.

'I suspect Richard was running drugs between here and the Indonesian coast, but the police haven't told me and I don't ask. When they were killed, the authorities in Asia contacted Oliver Bromley via his business manager—your Lyle—and asked him what to do about his grandchild. Mayberry agreed reluctantly on Bromley's behalf to pay for the child's maintenance.'

'But not to—to bring her home to Australia?' Beth faltered, and Kell shook his head.

'No way. I gather there was some reluctance even to pay for her keep. Anyway, Katie was finally placed in an orphanage overseas. She'd been there for six months when her grandfather died. When that happened, maintenance stopped being paid immediately. Mayberry obviously felt no responsibility for the child after Bromley's death. Then… Well, when the money ran out the authorities contacted the Australian police—and after some searching they contacted me as Katie's nearest relative. I flew over and brought her home.'

'So you didn't even know Christine had been killed until after Oliver Bromley died?' Beth asked quietly, and Kell shook his head again with a bleakness that told Beth his words were absolute truth.

'I knew nothing. I didn't even know Katie existed,' he said harshly. 'If I'd known…'

Beth looked wonderingly across at him. 'And you loved Christine,' she said softly, knowing that this too was the truth. There was something in this man's face that was making Beth believe she knew him. She could understand the deep hurt within. The knowledge was indefinable but it was there, for all she didn't understand it. 'You loved your half-sister.

Despite not seeing her for all that time, her death hurt. Didn't it?'

Kell looked out into the setting sun and the pain on his face was real and bitter to see. 'Christine was born when I was nine, after my mother had remarried someone I didn't like. My father was unhappy and bitter, and my mother was preoccupied with her new family. Christine was something...*someone* I could care for in the fairly bleak times I spent with my mother.

'I still spent most of my time with my father, up here in the mountains, so I didn't see Christine often. Then, when Christine was seven, my stepfather took a job in the States and I hardly saw Christine again. But, yes—I loved her, and I'll care for Katie for Christine's sake.'

'You mean you'll fight for Katie's inheritance?'

Kell grimaced.

'I don't give a toss about the two million dollars,' he said savagely. 'As you can see, I have more than enough to keep Katie. But your fiancé...'

'Lyle is not my fiancé,' Beth said steadily. 'I won't marry him if it will hurt Katie. No way.'

'Regardless of whether he's your fiancé or not, the man who did all the dealings with the overseas authorities when Katie's parents were killed wasn't Oliver Bromley,' Kell continued, his voice laced with distaste. 'It was his business manager— Lyle Mayberry.

'Bromley was an old man, and failing even then. And Mayberry...Mayberry only started working for him a few months before his death. Under his care all Bromley's old retainers—the housekeeper, the farm manager and anyone else close to the old man—were dispensed with. They weren't remembered in Bromley's will even though they'd been with the old man for forty years or more. Mayberry inherited the lot.'

'And…and Katie?'

'Mayberry didn't want anything to do with Katie either,' Kell told her. 'On Bromley's behalf, Mayberry refused point-blank to do anything more for Katie than he had to. He refused to bring her back to Australia—he argued that because her parents had resident status in Asia he didn't have to fund her return—and then he paid the absolute basic amount to keep her in the cheapest orphanage he could find.

'The health standards of the place where I found her were appalling. It's a wonder she wasn't dead—and I'm damned sure that's what Mayberry was hoping she soon would be. As I've said, after Bromley died the funding was cut off entirely, as if Mayberry had washed his hands of her. The law doesn't stipulate that grandchildren must be provided for, so Katie was left to rot.'

'Oh, no…' Beth looked back through the screen at the child playing with fierce concentration with the blocks. The child seemed so utterly alone—and here was the reason. Lyle…

'But Lyle…' Beth's mind was working cautiously through the sequence of events. 'Do you think Lyle could have used…what do they call it…undue duress to influence the will?'

'You know your cousin,' Kell said harshly. 'What do you think?'

There was only one answer to that. 'I think he did,' Beth said definitely. 'For Lyle to devote himself to a dying old man…' She shook her head. 'There's only one reason he'd do that—and that reason's money.' She sighed and met Kell's eyes defiantly. 'So you've kidnapped me to punish Lyle,' Beth whispered. 'I start to see.'

'It's simpler than that.' Kell Hallam rose then, and crossed to stare out at the mountains in the distance. 'More direct, if you like. All Christine and Richard's possessions were returned to Oliver Bromley when they were killed. When I went to find Katie I located the authorities who'd sent the possessions home. I found a very concerned officer—the one who'd taken all the trouble to contact Oliver and get Katie provided for—and he told me there was a household full of things. Christine had been a hoarder, despite her travelling.

'There were photographs—books and books of them—hand stacks of personal items. The officer had sent them all to Oliver Bromley after Katie had been placed in the orphanage, so I had my lawyer write a letter on Katie's behalf asking for them to be sent to her.'

'And were they?' Beth swallowed, knowing already what the answer would be. Lyle had been the sort of child to pull wings off flies and watch them suffer. For him to sort through an old man's possessions and find photographs...family mementoes... No.

'You know already,' Kell said slowly, watching Beth's face. 'You know the sort of man you were marrying. Mayberry sent a curt note to my lawyer saying Katie had no right to anything. As soon as the old man's possessions became his legally— after he was married to you—anything of value would be sold at public auction and the rest burned. He said he'd notify us of the auction details and Katie could bid like anyone else.'

Beth could just see Lyle writing that letter. She could *see* it. He would have enjoyed it immensely. A frail creature he could crush...

'That one letter...' Kell said implacably. 'That one letter cost him two million dollars. I'd seen the orphanage to which he'd consigned Katie. It was dreadful. No one there spoke English. No one thought Katie was anything more than a nuisance. There were much better places available for very little more money. And then...*then* your precious Mayberry was too mean to search for a photograph so the child could remember her mother.

'I was so angry I decided I'd contest the will on Katie's

behalf, but when my lawyer checked the terms of the will he found I could do better. As Bromley's only living relative, Katie stands to gain much more than her photographs if Mayberry fails to marry—and I'll do anything in my power to make sure Mayberry doesn't gain a cent. My lawyer tells me that as Katie's trustee I can make provision for Bromley's old housekeeper and farm manager on the basis that Katie had family obligations to them—but no such obligation would exist towards Mayberry.'

Kell sighed and shook his head, then turned to face her. 'So...I'm depriving your fiancé of two million dollars. And you...do you blame me?'

'Of course I don't blame you,' Beth told him. She rose as well and followed Kell to the edge of the verandah. Tentatively she laid a hand on his bare arm and felt a tremor of warmth run through her fingers from the touch. 'You must believe me that I didn't know. I never would have...'

'I can see that now.' Kell pulled away from her and stood, looking down at Beth in the fading light. 'It'd take a fool to think you're like him. But what the hell were you thinking of to agree to marry him?'

'I told you. I was desperate.'

'Are the lives of a few wallabies and possums worth marrying such a man?'

'I think they are,' Beth said stolidly. 'Since my parents died my animals have been the only things I could trust. To you they must seem nothing, but to me... Well, their lives are worth everything to me. Mr Hallam, there are things that are worth far more than money—maybe in the same way you think a few photographs are worth a jail sentence on a charge of kidnapping and imprisonment. You know you risked that?'

'I know,' he said heavily. 'I weighed it up—and found my anger was too great for me to do anything else.'

'And what would Katie have done if you'd gone to jail?'

Kell shook his head, and the same look of fatigue that Beth had noticed previously settled back heavily on his face.

'Heaven knows. But…' He shook his head. 'I don't know… A foster home? She's not happy here and I don't know what the hell to do. She's not—'

He broke off and Beth frowned.

'Not what?' Her head cocked sideways and she pursed her lips in thought. 'You told me before that Kate was mute. Why on earth did you say that?'

'Because she is.' Kell frowned. 'She's never spoken.'

'She spoke to me.'

'You were dreaming,' Kell said roughly. 'She hasn't talked. She didn't speak all the time she was in the orphanage overseas. Like I said, no one there spoke English, but some of the staff tried to communicate with her and they said she never tried to talk. Not once. And she's never said a word to me and she's been with me for three weeks.'

'She spoke to me,' Beth said firmly. 'She told me she missed her mother.'

Kell Hallam stared.

'She also told me her mother calls her Katie-bell, and that her mother made the pinafore she's wearing,' Beth told him. 'She said her mother made it on a sewing machine.'

Silence.

Inside, the child was concentrating fiercely on her blocks. The tiny clinks as each block fitted against the other sounded loud in the stillness of twilight.

'My mother sewed,' Kell said at last. 'She was a beautiful seamstress, and Christine…even when she was seven, Christine used to help her. I remember them both at the sewing machine. My mother had Christine making simple clothes right from the start.' He took a deep breath. 'And the pinafore…

'Katie was wearing it when they took her to the orphanage.

She had to wear the orphanage clothes there, but she carried
the pinafore like another child would carry a teddy bear. And
when I brought her here—her first morning—she put it on and
I haven't been able to put her in anything else. I take it away
while she's asleep and wash it. The damned thing's almost
falling apart, but she won't be parted from it.'

'I don't blame her,' Beth said softly. 'Not when it's the
only link she has…' She shook her head. 'Oh, Kell…Mr
Hallam…I'm so sorry. So very, very sorry.'

'There's no need for you to be sorry,' Kell said roughly, a
trace of emotion running strongly through his voice. 'It isn't
your look-out. Your cousin lied to you and you believed him.
As long as you don't marry him now there's no real damage
done.'

'There might already be damage,' Beth whispered. 'There
must be. For Lyle to leave that little girl over there all
alone…for him to abandon her…' Her fingers clenched into
her palms. 'I wish…oh, I wish…' She stopped and looked up
at Kell Hallam, to find him watching her with a curious look
in his eyes. She shook her head as though shaking away a bad
dream.

'You'll—you'll punish him, though,' she faltered. 'If you
take away…two million dollars, is it? For Lyle to have that
much money in his grasp and lose it…I can't think of a better
punishment. Not one that would hurt him more.' She hesitated.
'You are sure he can't inherit now? There's no other way?'

'I had my lawyer check and double check,' Kell told her.
'To marry in Australia you must register intention four weeks
before, and there are no exemptions. With less than two weeks
to go before he turns thirty, it's impossible for Mayberry to
get himself overseas to find himself a fast bride—we checked,
and the red tape would make it impossible—and Bromley's
will is very clear.

'It's a simple will, made at the last minute—my lawyer

suspects it was made when the old man was too ill to realise fully what he was doing—but it's watertight. *"Everything I possess to Lyle Mayberry on the condition that he is legally married by his thirtieth birthday."* That's all it says, so if he's *not* married it's as if Bromley never made a will and Katie inherits everything.'

'And if anything happens to Katie?' Beth asked slowly, watching the child again. Visions of her cousin and his ruthlessness appeared before her and she shuddered inwardly. 'If Katie had died over in that orphanage…'

'That's what Mayberry wanted to happen, I'm sure,' Kell told her. 'But if it had, still nothing changes for Mayberry. If he doesn't marry, regardless of Katie, then the money reverts to the public trustee. Mayberry still doesn't inherit.'

Kell shrugged. 'My half-sister and Richard weren't legally married, and that's one of the reasons Oliver Bromley lost contact with his son. Richard acknowledged Katie as his daughter, but Oliver Bromley never conceded he had a grandchild. I can only speculate as to whether that's the reason Oliver put Mayberry's marriage stipulation into his will.'

'Okay.' Beth took a deep breath, half relieved. If the money wouldn't revert to Lyle, then Katie was safe. There was only a small part of Beth whispering to her that Katie *would* have been at risk if she'd stood between Lyle and two million dollars—but it was a loud part all the same. 'So where does that leave me?' she asked slowly. She hesitated. 'Mr Hallam, you can't keep me here now.'

Beth looked up into Kell's troubled face and her heart twisted in a sudden, surprising pang at the thought of walking away from this man and this child and their troubles.

She had no business feeling such a pang. Kell Hallam was nothing to do with her and nor was the child. Nothing…

Why did it seem as if he was? Why was her heart going out to this man and this child?

'Of course I can't keep you here,' Kell was saying. 'You have your precious animals…' He paused. 'The only thing is, Beth, that you'll have to cope with your cousin's anger. You'll have to face Mayberry. How will he react to you jilting him?'

This time Beth couldn't repress her inward shudder, and Hallam saw it. His eyebrows snapped together. 'You're afraid of him?'

'I…no.' Beth gave herself an angry mental shake. Her problems with her cousin were her own. This man had enough worrying him without facing Lyle's anger on Beth's behalf, and Beth couldn't burden him further. She gave a weak smile. 'Lyle's been angry with me before,' she said firmly. 'I've survived.'

She'd only just survived. Some of the more dreadful examples of Lyle's temper tantrums over the years had left Beth with more than just emotional scars. Lyle was a lot older than Beth and had thoroughly enjoyed having a younger, smaller and altogether defenceless child sharing his house. Still, that was nothing to do with Kell Hallam.

'Then Katie and I will drive you home tomorrow,' Kell told her, watching her face across the shadows.

Beth didn't protest. There was nothing for her to do now but to go calmly home and await the results of Lyle's fury.

'You'll bring Katie with us in the car?' she asked, trying to focus her thoughts on something more pleasant. 'You didn't bring her when you…'

'When I kidnapped you?' Kell's mouth twisted into a rueful smile. 'I have a friend who's a photographer. He's the one who lent me the equipment. Keith told me if I was to be believable as a society photographer I had to act casual. Even so, Keith decreed Katie at my side would be a touch unbelievable. I had my housekeeper stay and babysit Katie until I returned.

'Mrs Scott was puzzled, to say the least, when I made it

clear I wanted the house to myself while you were here, but it can't be helped. I left you in the car when we arrived to give her time to leave without her seeing you in your bridal attire. Otherwise she'd have had kittens on the spot.' Kell's smile deepened. 'But may I say, Miss Beth Lister, that I approve of your jeans much more than I approve of your wedding dress. Satin's not your style.'

'I know it's not.' Beth chuckled. 'It was awful, but bridal splendour was what Lyle demanded.'

'Lyle demands a lot.'

'Yes.' Beth hesitated, looking in at the child on the floor. The possum was stirring again at her breast. 'Mr Hallam...'

'Kell.'

'Kell...if you'll excuse me,' she said softly, 'I need to feed my possum again, and...to be honest...I'm hungry myself. I'll go round to my quarters for the night.'

'No.'

'No?' Beth looked enquiringly up at him and frowned at the look of anger on his face. 'But...why not?'

'You're my guest, Beth,' Kell told her gently. 'I've treated you damnably—kidnapping you against your will and bringing you here as if you were some sort of criminal. You'll let me make some sort of reparation now.'

'Such as?'

'Such as letting me make you dinner,' he told her. He glanced at his watch. 'Go and feed your baby and come back here in half an hour. Katie and I will be waiting.'

Katie and I...

Beth fed her baby in silence, but her head was whirling in confusion.

Katie and I...

It was as if they were a family. He and Katie. Kell Hallam spoke as if he and the child were an established family, yet they were so disparate… The child wasn't speaking and Kell Hallam didn't know what on earth to do with her. Beth could see that at a glance. The child was deeply unhappy and Kell wasn't reaching her.

How could he cope with this emotionally scarred child? How would Kell Hallam begin to build a bridge to reach her? Kell spoke as if he was ready to assume responsibility for this orphaned child for the rest of her life—yet how could he?

Maybe there was a woman somewhere—a girlfriend—potential wife—ready to share the responsibility and make the idea of a family so much more possible.

What sort of woman would marry Kell Hallam?

Any sort at all, Beth thought grimly as she settled the little possum into its pouch again. The man was in his thirties—high time for him to be seeking a wife. He was rich and he was madly attractive. Somewhere there would be a woman. There had to be.

So why did he seem so alone? That was how he seemed—desperately alone. It was almost as if Kell needed Katie as much as the child needed him.

There were things going on here that didn't make any sense at all, Beth decided. She stared at herself in the mirror, wondering vaguely whether to change for dinner, but she decided against it. She had no wish to try and impress Kell Hallam. She was here unwillingly and tomorrow she'd leave this place and never see either man or child again. Beth had nothing to do with Kell Hallam. She was nothing to do with Katie.

They were a family and she—Bethany Lister—was an outsider.

The thought left her feeling chilled to the bone.

CHAPTER FIVE

KELL HALLAM could cook. Beth smelled the dinner before she was halfway round the verandah and her nose twitched in appreciation.

The wedding had been scheduled for early afternoon. She'd been far too nervous to eat lunch, she couldn't remember breakfast and now her stomach was sending its own urgent messages.

The smell of Kell's cooking answered these messages in full. Beth opened the French windows into the kitchen and sighed with pure gastronomic pleasure.

'Oh, yum.'

Then she hesitated.

Katie was still seated where Beth had left her half an hour ago—on the floor in the corner of the room. The child didn't look up as Beth entered. Beth looked closely at what she was doing and frowned in concern. The same tower of blocks was being rebuilt over and over again in repetitive monotony. Katie had built this tower three times while Beth and Kell had talked on the verandah, and now it was being built again. How many times had it been rebuilt while Beth hadn't been present?

Her attention was diverted by Kell. 'I hope you're not vegetarian.' Kell smiled but his smile was strained. He'd followed Beth's eyes as they rested on his small niece, and then he'd looked away again—as if what he saw there hurt. 'Beef Stroganoff and hot buttered noodles. Or just noodles and salad if you're vegetarian inclined.'

'If I was a vegetarian before I smelled this then I'd change on the instant.' Beth smiled across at him, allowing her attention to be diverted, as had been his intention. 'Where on earth did you learn to cook like this?'

'It was either learn to cook or starve when my mother walked out on my father,' Kell told her, his smile fading. 'My father had trouble boiling the kettle. He was the original creator of the macho ethic—men hunt and kill and women stay home in the kitchen and cook. I can understand in part why my mother walked out.'

'And you? Apart from your father you've been alone since then?' Beth asked. She followed Kell's example and also turned her attention totally from the child in the corner. If that was the way they were playing it, then it wasn't Beth's place to interfere.

'You mean, am I married?' Kell gave a short laugh which contained just a trace of bitterness. Maybe Beth had imagined it—or maybe she hadn't. 'No, Beth, there's no wife secreted in the next room. Or in any future room here, for that matter—unless it's a marriage of absolute convenience and nothing else.'

'Why not?' Beth asked curiously. She crossed to the wide bench beside the stove and hitched herself up to watch Kell as he stirred his wonderful-smelling concoction on the big Aga.

Beth's bare toes hung free from her frayed jeans, her legs too short to reach the floor. Perched in the warmth of the big kitchen, watching this man stir his pots, felt familiar and good. Like home. Like the home she hadn't had since she was tiny.

Beth was acting as if she was at home too—asking this man personal questions—but it didn't matter. Tomorrow she'd never see these two again. Bleak thought…

'I've seen what marriage does to people,' Kell said shortly, and Beth's eyebrows rose.

'What does it do to people?'

She was being impertinent here—but she would use impertinence or worse to drive her attention from the unhappy child in the corner!

'Marriage destroys them and it has the capacity to destroy those around them,' Kell said bluntly. 'I know that's just a personal belief, but you... I gather you must feel the same.'

'Why should I feel the same?' Beth asked, and waited while Kell tasted his brew and added a handful of herbs.

'You had no hesitation in agreeing to marry your cousin,' Kell told her thoughtfully—almost accusingly. 'Even though the marriage would have been in name only and marrying Mayberry would have precluded you from marrying anyone else.'

'That's different.'

'Why?'

'Because I'm just me. It's not that I disapprove of marrying—but who on earth would marry me?' Beth said the words before she thought, then, as they emerged, she could have bitten her stupid tongue. Stupid... Her statement sounded as if she were self-pitying—which was the last thing she was. 'Because I'm...I'm content on my own and I know my place is with my animals,' she faltered.

'Your place...?'

'It's true,' she said calmly, gathering her thoughts. 'I'm only ever at home when I have my farm and my animals. That's where I belong.'

'But you don't think like I do about marriage?'

'I haven't ever really considered marriage,' Beth said truthfully. 'It doesn't come into my plans.' She grinned. 'What man would ever be content with sharing his bed with me and my menagerie? But, no, I don't think like you do about marriage. I remember my parents as happy and I remember us as a family. It felt...it felt good.'

'But your parents' death ended your family life before you

can remember properly?' Kell asked, though he already knew the answer, and Beth nodded with reluctance.

'Yes. I was smaller than Katie. But I still remember my parents. They're still very important to me—which is why I think Katie's pinafore and the photographs you're trying to get for her are so important.'

She glanced back at the little girl on the floor. The child was so alone.

She couldn't bear it. In sudden decision Beth swung herself off the bench. She crossed to where the little girl sat mechanically building, knelt and firmly removed the blocks from the child's listless hands. 'Katie-bell, you've finished building your tower. Would you let me help you make something new?'

The child looked up with wide, apathetic eyes and said nothing.

'I'm making a car,' Beth said with firmness. 'You can watch me play while Uncle Kell finishes dinner.'

Silence.

'It won't work,' Kell told her softly.

'It won't work if I don't try,' Beth said grimly—and started building.

Beth's car was almost a respectable representation, but the child didn't help at all.

Katie's eyes watched Beth—not the growing car. Instead of interest there was a lacklustre waiting quality about the watching—as though she was waiting to see how long Beth's patience would last.

Beth simply ignored the apathy and kept on building.

'It's a Mercedes,' she told the child solemnly. 'Like your Uncle Kell's. I know your Uncle Kell's car is black, but I bet he wishes it was red with yellow stripes. A proper building-block artist is allowed to choose her own colours. It's called artistic licence.'

No response. Nothing.

Kell finished his casserole just as Beth's garish automobile had its last wheel added. He spooned the meal out onto two plates and a bowl—and then carried the bowl over to give Katie her meal where she sat on the floor.

Beth looked up, astounded.

'Are we all eating on the floor?' she demanded, and Kell gave a rueful smile.

'Katie won't eat while we watch. We'll eat at the table. She eats on her own.'

'Well, that's ridiculous,' Beth said roundly. She looked up at the table, to where Kell had set two places, complete with silver cutlery, linen table napkins and sparkling wine glasses. She took a deep breath and put down her car. 'Will you set another place, please, Mr Hallam?'

'But...'

Beth stood up and took Katie's bowl of food from Kell's hands. Instinctively she knew what she was doing was right. Katie had the look any one of Beth's wild creatures had when they were first brought to her. They cringed away in fear, and Katie was doing just that.

It wasn't that the child wanted to be on her own, Beth thought. It was just that she was afraid of being anything else. Who to trust? How could Katie tell after being abandoned by every adult she had ever depended on? 'Our Katie-bell's been alone for far too long,' Beth said softly. 'It's time her loneliness ended.'

She placed Katie's bowl down on the table, lifted her possum pouch from underneath her shirt and, in sudden decision, removed the pouch from over her head. Then she hung her little possum round Kell Hallam's neck.

After an involuntary exclamation of surprise, Kell submitted without question. He bent his head to her touch and Beth felt her hands give an unconscious start at the feel of his rough curls beneath her fingers.

'My possum needs a heartbeat,' she told him, her voice faltering just the smallest bit. 'Will you…give her yours?'

'While you do what with yours?' Kell was staring at Beth with bemusement. Involuntarily, it seemed, his hand slipped the small leather pouch down under his shirt to lie against his chest. His eyes twinkled in appreciation of Beth's sleight of hand. She'd handed over her responsibility almost before he could argue.

'I'm giving Katie mine,' Beth told him, trying not to watch the brown skin and hard muscular frame under his open shirt. 'And I'll show you how to hold your niece, so tomorrow, Mr Hallam, you can start being Katie's family.'

Then she stooped down beside the silent Katie and with one fluid movement caught the child's limp body up into her arms. The child was underweight for her age and ridiculously small—there was nothing of her—and her body quivered against Beth's like a captive bird. Beth held her tight in the space just vacated by her possum and lowered both of them onto a chair at the kitchen table.

'Katie and I are ready for dinner now, Mr Hallam,' she said solemnly to Kell. 'If you'll be so kind as to play waiter.' Then she looked across to the bench, where Kell had poured a plastic beaker of milk. 'And Katie-bell would like her milk in a wine glass,' she said definitely. 'She's one of us, Mr Hallam. We're eating together.'

'Your possum is wriggling,' Kell said, bemused. 'It tickles.'

'Lucky you.' Beth grinned. 'There's a lot of men who'd give their back teeth to be tickled while they eat.'

'Yeah? On whose authority do you have that?'

'I decided it myself,' Beth admitted, her smile broadening at the look on Kell's face as he felt the little creature move.

'You've just got to believe me—because you have no choice at all!'

It was the strangest meal Beth had ever eaten—but also the nicest.

Kell's Beef Stroganoff was absolutely delicious. Luckily the beef, onions and tiny button mushrooms were all in bite-sized pieces, lying in their lovely creamy sauce on a bed of noodles in such a way that made eating with a fork easy. With her free hand Beth held Katie so close she could feel the child's heart—as she intended the child to feel hers.

For the first five minutes of the meal the child ate nothing—simply sat and watched—but after her first few mouthfuls Beth paused.

'Would you like me to feed you, Katie-bell?'

There was a resolute shake of the small pigtails. Beth kept on eating, her eyes sending an urgent message to Kell not to interfere. He didn't—just calmly kept eating himself—and Beth blessed him for his perception. The child had to believe that she was being cherished, but also she had to feel that no one cared whether she ate or not. Katie wouldn't be forced to do anything against her will.

And finally Katie ate. As Beth finished her casserole, and started concentrating on the really excellent wine Kell had poured for her, one small hand reached out and lifted a spoon. The other hand linked somehow in the folds of Beth's T-shirt and stayed entangled.

This new contact wasn't all bad, the hand proclaimed, and as the child ate her first spoonful, and then her second, the tension round the table dissipated.

'How long does your little possum need a heartbeat?' Kell asked curiously as Katie reached cautiously for her wine glass of milk. The child stiffened—and then realised the question had nothing to do with her. She relaxed again and started drinking.

'If I was at home I might leave her in a heated pouch away from me tonight,' Beth told Kell. 'She coped well with her bout of freedom on the lawn. She still needs a pouch, though. At the farm I have electric blankets looped into the lining of pouches so my babies can stay warm when I no longer carry them.'

'I see.' He looked as if he didn't see at all. Kell Hallam sat over his wine, the baby possum at his breast, and he looked for all the world like someone on quicksand. Clearly he was totally at a loss.

Finally Katie finished her meal. The child had eaten everything in her bowl, Beth noted with satisfaction, but still she hadn't spoken. Beth herself was starting to doubt whether she'd heard the child speak at all.

'Now it's bedtime, Katie-bell,' Kell said gently, and the child flinched. The hand clutching Beth gripped tighter.

'I think I'll go to bed now, too,' Beth told the pair of them. She rose and put Katie onto her feet. The hand still clutched, preventing Beth from straightening. Beth tried to disengage the hand, the hand gripped tighter—and after a moment she lifted the child again.

Beth looked doubtfully up at Kell. What to do here? Walk away from this unassailable need?

Beth could no sooner do that than she could abandon one of her injured creatures. It went against everything her heart was telling her was right.

'Where do you sleep, sweetheart?' she asked, and the child's face burrowed into Beth's shoulder and stayed there, out of sight.

'Katie has a bedroom just next to mine,' Kell said heavily. 'She doesn't like it, though. Katie's been here for three weeks and most nights she's ended up out here on the floor.'

'You don't let her sleep in with you?' Beth asked gently, and Kell shook his head.

'Hell, no.' He ran a hand through his hair in a gesture Beth was starting to recognise. Then he sighed. 'I don't know whether you can imagine, but…do you realise the trouble I had bringing Katie into the country? Katie's a US citizen with residency status in Asia. I'm her mother's half-brother. I'd never met Katie before and Katie's parents had never applied to have Katie take Australian citizenship.

'So…I had to convince our social welfare people that I was the only person willing to take Katie on, that she had a right to come back to Australia, and—hardest of all—that I was an honest, well-intentioned bloke whose only concern was for Katie's welfare. They were all for treating me like I was some sort of pervert.

'Katie sleeps in her own room, Miss Lister, and that's an end to it. Anything else and the welfare officers will take Katie away from me.'

'I see,' Beth said slowly, turning the problem over in her mind. She did see, too. For a single adult male to adopt a small girl… It went against every social convention.

The problems of social conventions, however, weren't helping Katie one bit. 'Where did you say she slept?' Beth asked cautiously, holding Katie close.

'I told you. In here. On the floor with her damned blocks. Oh, and with her pinafore. I make her put on pyjamas, but she goes to sleep holding the pinafore like a rag doll.'

'You've tried making a bed for her in here?'

'Of course I've tried,' Kell said heavily. 'It doesn't work. I don't know what her sleeping arrangements were in the orphanage, but she prefers bare floor.'

'I bet she doesn't,' Beth whispered, nuzzling the little girl's soft hair with her lips. 'I just bet you don't, Katie, love, but the stove's here, and the warmth, and a bedroom by yourself is a cold and scary place.' She bit her lip. 'Mr Hallam...'

'Kell.'

'Kell...' Beth swallowed. It was hard to call this man by his first name. It seemed too familiar by half—as if it was conceding an intimacy she felt but didn't want to acknowledge. 'Kell, do you have an electric blanket somewhere?'

'I've any amount of them. It gets cold up in the mountains in winter. But...'

'Then could we rig up a warm cocoon round Petal's pouch?'

'Petal?'

'Katie called the possum Petal,' Beth told him, smiling. 'Unless you want to sleep with my possum under your shirt—and I warn you she's looking for feeds every couple of hours—then I'd like to rig up a heated pouch.'

'I don't think I want to sleep with a possum at all,' Kell said bluntly. 'I'd roll on the damned thing. We'd have squashed possum and you'd sue me for squillions. But what about you?'

'I think...' Beth said slowly, and then hesitated. Katie was limp in her arms, but her small hand still clutched the front of Beth's T-shirt with its own urgent message. 'I think I have to reprioritise. I do it all the time when I get a new little creature. Decide whose needs are greater and how I can meet all requirements. And now...' She paused again and met Kell's eyes directly. 'Now I think I've decided whose needs take precedence.'

She pulled the child a little way from her and fixed her with a direct look. 'Katie-bell, your uncle's given me an absolutely enormous bed,' she said gravely. 'And it's really cold with just me in it. For tonight, will you share my bed?'

The child's eyes widened.

'I might wake you up every time I feed my possum,' Beth

warned. 'And if you snore I'll tickle you until you stop. But would you like to sleep with me and Petal?'

Still silence.

Beth bit her lip. She could just pick this waif of a child up and take her—but it was no use her taking this tiny child and comforting her through the night if nothing was to be gained by it. If Beth left tomorrow and Katie was still the same silent little person Kell had been fighting to understand, then Beth would have achieved nothing. Katie was making no contact at all with her uncle—and that had to change.

'Let me go, then, Katie-bell,' Beth told her softly. 'If you don't want to come and share a room with Petal and me for the night then I'll pop you back down with your blocks and you can sleep where you normally sleep. But otherwise…otherwise you'll have to turn round and tell your uncle Kell that you want to stay with me tonight.'

Silence.

'Okay, then, Katie,' Beth said calmly, as if Katie had made a decision and it didn't make one whit of difference to Beth. 'If that's the way you want it.' She started to put her down. The child clutched convulsively, but Beth's hands were firm as she set the child on her feet and put her away from her.

'If you've changed your mind…if you want to stay with me tonight—then, Katie, you'll have to tell your uncle Kell what you want,' Beth said softly. 'Do it, Katie.'

'What do you want, Katie-bell?' Kell asked, his voice grave. He stooped so his eyes were on the same level as his small charge's. 'Tell me.'

The child's eyes opened wide. She opened her mouth a couple of times but nothing came out. Her breathing deepened. There were obviously enormous pressures in this tiny mind. Enormous conflict. Beth's heart turned over. In a moment she'd break and take the child back in her arms. It took a

Herculean effort to hold herself still. But Kell took Katie's hands in his and held them, his eyes gentle.

'Tell me, Katie.'

The whole world held its breath.

And Katie broke. Her silence ended.

'I want Beth,' the child whispered. 'I want to stay with Beth.'

CHAPTER SIX

BETH woke to feed her possum at two a.m.

The possum wasn't stirring when she woke, but it was time it was fed. Beth felt down to where Kell had fashioned the pouch to hang at her bedside. Her hand slipped in and found the little creature sleeping snugly in heated bliss. Kell had gone to considerable trouble to make sure the pouch was heated just right—in fact, he'd slashed a full-size electric blanket and resoldered the circuitry while Beth had watched in dismay.

'Are you sure you know what you're doing?' she'd demanded. 'I have no wish for barbecued possum for breakfast.'

'Trust me.' Then he'd smiled with that damned treacherous smile that made Beth's heart do backflips. Trust him? She'd no sooner trust Kell Hallam than fly.

Still, at least his promise of a working pouch had been fulfilled. She disengaged Katie's sleepy hold on her nightgown, waited a moment until she was sure the child wouldn't wake and then rose to prepare the tiny bottle of formula.

It was too glorious a night to spend her time with the little possum inside. Katie had gone to sleep clutching Beth like a lifeline but was now deeply asleep. The French windows were beckoning. Beth slipped through with her furry burden, settled herself in one of Kell's wonderful chairs overlooking the garden and moonlit river beyond and started to feed.

Kell found her there five minutes later.

The man came up behind her like a ghost, and Beth almost jumped out of her skin when his tread sounded right behind her. As it was she gave a quickly stifled squeak. The little possum started, jerking away from the bottle in alarm. But the creature was only frightened for a moment. Petal gave Beth one angry glare, then reapplied herself to matters much more important than marauding males in the night.

'For heaven's sake,' Beth whispered crossly. 'Must you sneak around like a...like a sneak thief?'

'This is my home,' Kell said mildly, pulling up a chair beside Beth and lowering his long body onto the cushions. 'I can sneak anywhere I please.' He smiled, his smile half mocking in the moonlight. 'Apart from my ladies' bedroom, that is. I've declared your room out of bounds. There's quite a crew inside your bedroom, lady, and any more's a crowd. How are you finding your sleeping companions?'

'Nobody snores,' Beth reassured him, relaxing slightly as her alarm settled. 'At least, I might, but then I'm asleep so I can't hear me.'

'You don't snore,' Kell assured her, and watched Beth's expression change to a frown.

'But...how do you know that?' she asked cautiously. 'I thought you said our room was out of bounds for sneaking.'

Kell grinned and held up a hand, as if to placate forthcoming anger. 'I've been listening at your door, of course, though I promise I haven't opened it. You might have taken my responsibility from me but you can't stop me checking. I've been so accustomed to checking Katie every couple of hours over the past few weeks it's become a habit. It doesn't worry me,' he said quickly, seeing her look of concern. 'Like you, I'm accustomed to waking during the night for my animals. When I have a cow or horse in labour...'

'But... You didn't think Katie would settle with me?'

'She has bad dreams,' Kell admitted. 'That's why I listened at your door a few times. I thought...' He hesitated. 'Well, I wondered if you could cope. Try as I might, I haven't been very good at coping myself. I was starting to think—'

He broke off, and the silence of the night washed over them. There was only the gentle sucking slurps of the small creature in Beth's lap, dying to nothing now as the little possum reached saturation point and drifted towards sleep.

'You were starting to think?'

'I was starting to think I was a fool to believe I could care for her,' Kell said heavily, staring sightlessly out into the night. 'When I was first contacted and told of Katie's existence—well, all I thought of was that Katie was Christine's daughter and I was all the family she had now. But it's not enough. I might be all the family Katie has, but she needs a real family—and I'm not one. I'm not what she needs.'

He sighed. 'She spoke to you,' he said softly. 'She spoke. In one night you've done what I couldn't do in three weeks. It's made me see clearly how inadequate I am. It's made me see how hopeless keeping her here is.'

'So what are you suggesting?'

'The social welfare people have recommended a foster family might be more satisfactory for Katie,' he said heavily. 'They say a proper mother and father and maybe a sibling or two is what she needs, and they have grave doubts as to my long-term ability to parent her. They think I should still visit her—keep a link alive for her with Christine—but they doubt my suitability for long-term care.'

'You love her, though,' Beth said gently, watching his face in the moonlight. 'Surely that's the most important thing. Love… If you love her enough, Kell, then anything's possible.'

'Yeah?' He stood, then, gazing down at Beth in the soft rays of the moon. 'I guess you'd know that, wouldn't you, Beth? You know what love is. It's the Beth Lister specialty. You take in injured and orphaned creatures and love them and tend them until they heal. You put everything else aside—everything that normal women deem important—because car-

ing's the most important thing in the world.' He shook his
head. 'I don't know that I've ever met a creature like you in
my life. You're a half-wild creature yourself.'

Beth swallowed. She looked up at him and her heart gave
a painful twist. This man had needs of his own that weren't
being met. She could see them clearly. For all he was rich,
strong, sophisticated...

'Kell...'

She hesitated, and then rose to face him in the moonlight.
All of a sudden she was acutely conscious of the flimsy nightgown she was wearing. It was soft cotton but worn thin with
age, and she wasn't at all sure it was decent. Her hair hung
in soft tendrils down over her breasts, but her thick hair wasn't
enough cover at all. Kell Hallam was still wearing his moleskins and workshirt. Beside her, he seemed large, impregnable
and powerful. And in contrast Beth felt young, vulnerable and
very, very unsure.

But it was this man who was needing the help. This man
who was crying out a need...

'Kell, you just have to do what you think best,' she told
him gently. 'Follow your heart. Don't listen to what all these
officials are telling you. You love Katie. That's all that can
matter.' She put a hand on his arm and her eyes were huge
and pleading in the moonlight.

Kell mustn't give up his little girl. There was a part of Beth
that feared this man—feared the effect he had on her—but
there was another part of her that went straight out and met
his needs head-on. Put Katie in a foster home? No, no and no!
'You can do it,' she urged. 'You mustn't give up now.'

Kell looked down at her and his face changed. There was
a look in his eyes that Beth didn't understand. Confusion?
Doubt? Maybe both of those, and there was something else
now, that she didn't recognise. Beth took a step back and
watched him, her eyes fearful but gravely wondering.

And suddenly Beth knew at last what the emotion she was feeling was—and it scared her half to death.

'I have to go,' she managed to whisper. The little possum was still cradled in her spare hand, sated with milk and sleeping soundly. 'My possum needs his pouch and I...Kell, I need to go back to sleep.'

'Don't we all,' Kell said dryly. His hands came out and strongly caught her shoulders. 'Beth, don't look so scared. Maybe we can work something out here.'

'I don't know what you mean.'

'Did you say your farm was being sold?'

'I... Yes.' Beth swallowed. 'It is.'

'And without your cousin's money you can't buy it?'

'That's right.' The feel of Kell's hands on her shoulders was doing strange things to Beth. She felt strange... surreal...floating. As if this night were something out of time. Some strange dream that at any minute she would wake from. It was so hard to make her mind work. To make herself think of anything past his hands. Past the feel of him...

'So what will you do without your farm?'

Beth woke from her strange dream then. Reality slammed back with dreary horror. What was he saying? What would she do without her farm?

'I don't know,' she admitted. 'I'll find homes for my animals, I guess. Some other conservation carer... And then I'll...I suppose I'll go back to vet nursing.'

'What if I offered you a job?'

A job...

Beth bit her lip, trying hard to make herself concentrate on what this man was saying. Kell's hands were still on her shoulders and the eyes looking down at her were magnetic in their intensity.

'A...a job?' she whispered.

'Katie needs a woman to be with her,' Kell told her. 'I saw

that clearly tonight. She needs a mother substitute. She needs you.'

'You mean she needs a nanny?' Beth managed. She tried to take a step back, but Kell's hands held her fast.

'Not a normal nanny,' Kell told her. 'I already have a house-keeper. As I told you, Mrs Scott's usually here, but I gave her and all my other employees the next couple of weeks off while I thought I'd be holding you here against your will. Mrs Scott…well, she's a kindly soul, but she can't get any closer to Katie than I can. I can't see that any professionally qualified nanny would do any better. But you…'

'I'm not a nanny.'

'No. But you have a heart as big as this country. And, Beth…if I agreed to bring your menagerie here there's no reason why you can't keep right on doing the work you love. And Katie could help, and maybe…maybe in doing so she'd find her own healing.'

'Bring my animals?'

'It'd take some organisation,' Kell told her, thinking aloud. 'The dogs would have to be trained to leave your little patients alone, but that's no problem. I don't permit them to worry the local wildlife, and having wildlife closer to the house is just an extension of that. They're smart dogs—easily trained. We could fence off part of the garden and make a run out the back for your bigger creatures. The bush round here is thick and wild enough for your rehabilitation. Why wouldn't it work, Beth Lister?'

'It wouldn't…'

'Why not?'

'I don't… I don't…'

Beth faltered and stopped. Her heart was turning crazy som-ersaults and she couldn't think. She couldn't think past the feel of this man's hands on her shoulders—past the look in his eyes as he directed his compelling gaze straight at her.

'Why not, Beth?' he asked again, and the grip of his hands grew more urgent. 'Your heart's so big. Surely you could share your love with one little girl who needs you so desperately.'

'It wouldn't work. It just wouldn't,' she told him desperately. It was as much as Beth could do to make her tongue work. Her heart was still turning somersaults and she felt so giddy that if Kell's hands hadn't been holding her she might well have fallen.

'Tell me why?'

'I can't...'

There was a long silence. The moonlight was all around them, bathing them in its silver beams. Down below the house the river ran its deep and mysterious course, with the moon and stars reflecting on its mirrored surface.

Magic.

Magic was all around them. Enveloping them. Engulfing them so that Beth could no more pull away than she could speak. She stood powerless in this man's hold while his eyes devoured her—his hands holding her tighter and tighter until he suddenly pulled her gently close to his body.

And Beth couldn't resist. It was the night, she told herself desperately. It was the place. The moonlight. Anything except this man pulling her closer, holding her against his body with infinite tenderness so that the frail creature in Beth's hands was cradled between them with a warmth that was more secure than any pouch.

And Beth's face was wonderingly lifting up, her eyes widening in the moonlight as Kell's hand rose to cup her face—moving her so that his mouth could come down and kiss the lovely girl in his grasp.

It was a kiss of a sweetness that Beth had never felt before. It was a kiss of a sweetness that she hadn't known existed. As lips met lips a feeling swept through her like a shaft of light, burning into her body and making her piercingly aware of every inch of herself—every inch of this man's body against hers. She felt the floorboards of the verandah against her bare toes as she raised herself to meet Kell's kiss, and it was as if the floorboards were a curve that connected her to Kell. That held her close—that made her one.

And then she was lost. She knew it. One part of her was wholly centred on the kiss, but another part was screaming at her that she—Beth Lister—was tumbling head over heels into love with a man she had no knowledge of. With a man who wanted nothing of a permanent relationship. Who wanted nothing but a kiss.

It didn't matter. It couldn't matter. For now…for this magic moment there was only the feel of Kell's body against hers—the feel of his hands on her soft cheeks and the smell of him: raw and masculine and so…

She didn't know. She couldn't define the feeling. He was so—what? So much a part of her? Ridiculous thought, but there it was. It made sense. It felt like the truth. This man was a part of her. That was how she felt. That was how she'd felt the moment she'd looked out of the window back at the hotel and seen him all that time ago—or was it only a few short hours?

Surely not? Surely she couldn't have known this man only for hours? It felt as if she had always known him.

Beth opened her lips to deepen the kiss—deepen the feel of him—and a part of her rejoiced and a part of her reacted with overwhelming sadness.

This was something she'd never thought possible. To feel like this about any man…

And to feel like this about a man of wealth and power—a man who was trying to persuade her to work for him and who would use any means within his power to gain his ends…

Kell Hallam was ruthless. Beth had seen that only too well. A girl would be crazy to fall in love with him.

A girl already had.

All these thoughts were kaleidoscoping round and round in her mind, intensifying the sweetness of the kiss because of the knowledge of the pain that would follow. And sure enough, when Kell finally drew away, Beth felt pain slice through her like a red-hot sword. As if part of her was being torn apart.

It was crazy to let him touch her. Crazy, when she knew that only heartache could ensue.

Beth wasn't the sort of girl men fell in love with. Hadn't she been told that over and over again? 'Men will try to get you into their beds,' her aunt Hilda had told her, over and over again. 'But as for marrying you... Worthless child. Stupid girl. Get yourself a useful occupation if you can because that's all you're good for.' And when Lyle had announced he was marrying his cousin, Aunt Hilda had nearly had hysterics.

'There must be some other way you can get the money. To marry *her*...!'

'There's no one else stupid enough...'

So much for that. So much for the past. For now there was only the present—and Kell looking down at Beth in the moonlight with eyes that were gravely questioning.

There was no future with this man. Nothing but heartache if she let him closer. And what good would that do Katie? To let Katie become attached to her and then to leave because she was so in love with Kell that she couldn't bear it?

There was always a wrench when Beth released a wild creature—always a fleeting regret at lost affection. Now, though... The loss had to be now, before the tie had been created. It was kinder to cut herself off now. Kinder because if she grew any closer then to walk away would be impossible. And she had to walk away.

'That...that's why it wouldn't work,' she whispered unsteadily, reaching out to touch Kell's hand in a fleeting gesture that was as quickly withdrawn. 'Kell. I only have to look at you and I want to touch you. Call it crazy, but that's the way it is.' She took a deep breath and steadied. 'I guess you'd call it sex appeal or something. You must know you have it. And I don't want it, Kell. I don't want…entanglements.

'I'm free. That's what I always have been. That's the way I like it. And if I came here…then I couldn't walk away. It'd wrench my heart out. I couldn't love Katie and then leave when you decide you need another employee…or if you eventually marry and don't need me. I'm free, Kell. And I'm asking you to respect that. Leave me be, Kell. You've abducted me, and now it's time to set me free. You have a duty to do that.'

'Is that what you really want?'

'Of course it is,' she managed, in a voice that trembled as much as her heart. 'Of course it is. I need to be free.'

'Beth…'

'No.'

He reached out, but she put her hands up to ward him off. 'You abducted me,' she managed, in a voice that was strained to breaking. 'You've taken me against my will. It's not your right to seduce me to make me work for you. If you want a nanny for Katie, then you'll have to find one some other way. You have no right to try and persuade me in such a way. No right at all.'

And, before he could respond, she turned and walked back into her bedroom and closed the door behind her.

It was a long time before Beth slept, and when she did her dreams were strange and troubled. She fed the little possum again at five, and then fell asleep again to dreams that were even worse.

Morning saw Katie awake before Beth. The child lay passive beside her, eyes huge and infinitely patient as she waited for

Katie to stir.

Finally it was too much for the child. She put a cautious hand out and lifted Beth's eyelid.

Beth woke with a start—and managed a smile as she realised what was happening.

'Hey, Katie, I'm at home in here.' She smiled, the pain of the night receding in the face of the child's pixieish anxiety. 'There's no need to open my windows.'

And Katie chuckled. It was a soft, brief chuckle, but it was a chuckle for all that and Beth's heart went out to her. What a lovely sound.

I could make a difference with this child, she told herself. I could...

And walk away at the end of an employment contract? I don't think so.

It was all just too hard. Beth's arms went out to cradle the little girl against her, and for a moment she felt as forlorn as Katie must have felt, abandoned in her orphanage all those months ago.

'Let's get dressed,' she whispered bleakly, forcing herself to smile again. 'We'll have breakfast and then your uncle Kell's going to drive me home.'

'H-Home?' The little girl's voice was tremulous and husky from long months of disuse. 'But...where do you live?'

'I live on a farm a few miles away from here, Katie-bell,' Beth told her. 'I just came for a visit to you and your uncle. Today I have to go again.'

'Take me with you.'

'I can't do that.' Beth ruffled the little girl's soft hair and felt her heart wrench. 'But you'll see me again. I'll ask your uncle if I might visit whenever my animals don't need me. And today you're coming to my farm and you'll be able to see all my animals. You should see my little babies, Katie.

You'll love them. There's a baby koala who was rescued after a bushfire, and a great big daddy kangaroo who was hit by a car, and a little echidna...'

'What's an echidna?' Katie asked dubiously, and Beth chuckled.

'Now there's a tricky animal to explain to a little girl brought up in America and Asia. An echidna's a bit like a huge pincushion, Katie—a pincushion with the world's biggest nose. You just wait until you see him. I think you'll say he's cuter even than a koala. Now...let's get dressed. What would you like to wear today?'

'My pinafore.'

Of course.

The pinafore was the child's only security. Adults had nothing to do with long-term safety in this little girl's experience. And Beth had to go...

CHAPTER SEVEN

KELL wasn't in the house when they went to find him.

The house was deserted when, dressed, the girls took themselves off to investigate. For the first time since she'd found her, Beth left her little possum behind, confident now that Petal was coping beautifully in the heated pouch Kell had made. But where was Kell? There was no one in the garden or anywhere in sight of the house. There was no sound from the dogs. Nothing.

'We'll have to call,' Beth told Katie, but Katie wouldn't. Since Beth had said she was leaving she'd lost her smile. She clung to Beth's hand in silent apathy.

Finally Beth took her into the kitchen and found a note on the table.

Gone down to the bottom paddock to feed the cattle. I'll see you back here at nine—if you're up by then, you pair of sleepyheads.

'Your uncle is very rude, Katie-bell,' Beth told the child, reading her the note and managing a smile. She hesitated, trying to resist the impulse to voice her thought. What harm could it do? She was leaving today. What harm would it do to see all of Kell that she could? 'Maybe we could go and see what he's doing,' she said carefully. 'Do you know where the bottom paddock is?'

Katie considered, and for a moment Beth thought she might retire back into the defensive silence of the night before, but it seemed the silence was broken permanently. 'Every morning

91

he gives hay to the cows on the other side of the river,' Katie told her. 'There's a bridge. I know a short cut if you want to go that way—but you need to wear gum boots.'

'Why do I need to wear gum boots?' Beth asked cautiously, and Katie momentarily lost her apathy.

'Because of Joe Blakes.'

Joe Blakes. Snakes. Beth grinned down at Katie's shy smile. 'Well, well.' She chuckled. 'You sound almost Australian. Joe Blakes, indeed! What else has your uncle been teaching you about our Australian language?'

Katie looked pleased. She smoothed down her pinafore with a self-conscious smile, as though about to recite something carefully learned. The child had obviously been taking everything in over the past few weeks, even though she hadn't spoken.

'Well...I don't go to the bathroom any more,' she stated carefully. 'I go...I go to the dunny. And we feed the chooks instead of feeding the hens. Uncle Kell calls me mate sometimes, instead of Katie. That's Australian, I reckon and "I reckon" is Australian too. And Mrs Scott said the girl who came to the door selling dead flowers had a kangaroo loose in her top paddock. So...I'm learning all the time.'

'I see you are.' Beth laughed and swept Katie up in her arms to give her a swift hug. 'Now... Do you want to come and find your Uncle Kell? I don't have gum boots—but we'll sing all the way.'

'Sing?' Katie stared. 'Why will we sing?'

'Well, Joe Blakes are more scared of us than we are of them,' Beth assured her. 'And if they hear me singing "Ten Green Bottles" they'll be heading for the outback before we reach the end of the garden. Now, Katie-bell, are you sure you can find your Uncle Kell?'

'Yes,' Katie assured her. 'It's easy.'

It wasn't.

Beth had packed one pair of light sneakers as her only non-bridal footwear. They were very clearly inadequate. Beth set off down through the garden with the gum booted Katie, singing all the time as a Joe Blakes precaution, but when they hit the banks of the river she stopped dead.

'Katie…'

'The bridge is along here,' Katie assured her, tugging Beth's hand in protest at Beth's stopping. 'We could have come down along the road but it takes ages. Uncle Kell says this way's the best.'

Uncle Kell might, Beth thought, staring with dismay at the riverbank, but if he really thought that, then the man must have webbed feet. They had emerged on the riverbank a hundred yards from the bridge, and the ground between where they stood and the bridge was sloppy, sodden, river flat. Smooth mud…

'Katie, I don't have gum boots,' Beth said carefully, eyeing the plane of shiny mud with misgivings.

'I told you we needed them.'

'You said I needed them for Joe Blakes.'

'You need them for mud as well.' Katie giggled. She seized Beth's hand and tugged. 'Come on, Beth. Please… Uncle Kell says it's sort of fun sinking, and it looks delicious.'

'Delicious…' Beth stared out over the mud and despite her qualms she felt the corners of her mouth twitch into a smile. Delicious… Maybe…

'Katie-bell, I'll get all muddy.'

'It doesn't matter. It doesn't.'

And maybe it didn't. Katie tugged with dogged determination. Beth hesitated for all of thirty seconds, grinned to herself, hauled off her sneakers and let Katie lead on. After all, it did look such glorious mud. She took one step forward, and then another…and then another…

Katie, light on her feet and feather-weight, sank a couple

of inches at each step. Beth sank to her ankles on her first step, the lovely smooth mud squelching up in streams between each bare toe. On the second step Beth sank to her calf and on the third to her knees. Beth pulled one foot out of its sucking, squelching hole to take another crazy step forward, and by the time she'd gone ten yards she was coated with black slime and helpless with laughter.

'Ugh, you horrible child. I'll be stuck here for ever… Ugh, Katie…' And then she looked down at her companion's innocent face and paused. 'Where on earth are you taking me, Katie-bell? Does your Uncle Kell really bring you this way? You tell me the truth, now.'

'No,' Katie admitted, giving a silly chuckle and tugging Beth on. 'But he showed me the mud from the bridge and told me he used to come this way when he was my age. He said his mum used to chuck a wobbly whenever he did—but I don't know what chucking a wobbly means. Uncle Kell promised me that on the day I started talking again he'd bring me down here as a celebration. I was too scared to ask him last night. But this morning I thought that I'd talked and talked, and last night I even talked to Uncle Kell. So I thought I'd bring you.'

'Gee, thanks.' Beth completed one oozy step and started another. 'And I must remember to thank your Uncle Kell for giving you the idea. If ever we get to him, that is.'

'You can do it if you try,' Katie said blithely. 'Look at me. I'm not even getting my pinafore dirty. With my gum boots on, I'll stay clean as a whistle.'

Which was more than could be said for Beth. Fifty yards further on Beth paused for breath. She'd slipped twice and put a hand down to save herself, going elbow-deep in mud in the process. Now she resembled nothing so much as a war victim, recently escaped from the trenches.

Beth stared out over the river flat. They'd gone about half-way. Ahead of them, the mud was a shiny smooth plane, glimmering in the morning sun with benign beauty. A couple of sandpipers were scurrying along the water's edge, their tiny webbed feet hardly leaving an impression on the mud. In contrast, where Beth walked there were holes that looked as if a pile driver had been mud-hopping.

'Katie, I don't think I'll have the strength to get all the way to the bridge across the mud flats,' Beth gasped, fighting for breath. 'There must be an easier way to do th—'

'There is.'

Beth stopped mid-sentence. She stared up along the river in stupefaction—to find Kell Hallam standing on the bridge above them, his eyes alight with amusement.

'Morning, girls,' Kell called, his voice so bland Beth just knew he was trying hard not to laugh. 'Taking a mud bath for your complexions?'

At Beth's side, Katie's hand tightened its grip. There was still an element of distrust here, Beth knew, and fought down her own reaction to Kell as she responded to the child's needs. Maybe Katie hadn't had very much to do with her father—or with men at all. She was certainly responding much more easily to Beth than she was to her Uncle Kell.

Beth stared up at the man on the bridge and she could surely understand Katie's disquiet—though maybe her own distrust of Kell sprang from a different source. He was in jeans this morning, with a torn checked shirt open almost to the waist. The sun glinted on his hair; she could see the smile in his eyes even from here, and the sight of the man's bare, muscled chest and strongly boned frame made Beth's toes quiver under the mud all by themselves.

Stupid girl! Stupid, stupid reaction! What on earth was she thinking of? Beth stood as fast as she could in such a ridiculous situation and glared for all she was worth.

'I gather you suggested Katie might come this way,' she

managed breathlessly. 'Thank you, Mr Hallam. You'll pay my dry cleaning bill, of course?'

'There's a cheaper solution to that, too,' he smiled. 'Are you still wearing your possum?'

'My possum is safely home in bed,' Beth retorted. 'Sensible possum.'

'Then you have no problems.' Kell grinned. 'I assume you can swim?'

'I don't...'

'You don't swim?' Kell shook his head. 'I don't believe you, Miss Lister. You have the look of a woman who can swim like a fish. However, if you say so...' He turned his attention to his small niece. 'Our Miss Lister appears to be a damsel in distress, Katie-bell. We need a plan. How about if your uncle Kell saves her?'

Katie-bell stared up at him in confusion. The little girl looked from her Uncle Kell to Beth and then back again. 'I don't know whether Beth wants to be saved,' the child managed, clutching Beth tighter.

'Nonsense. Maidens in distress always want to be saved,' Kell said firmly, his smile growing more wicked by the minute. 'Have you ever read of a valiant knight rescuing his fair damsel from the very teeth of a fire-breathing dragon only to have the maiden say, "Sorry, dear, I'm rather enjoying my barbecue"? That's ridiculous. In fairy stories, it's simply not done to refuse to be rescued, so I don't see why Beth should refuse either.'

Katie stared up, open-mouthed. She gaped for all of ten seconds and then, to Beth's amazement, Katie giggled.

'We haven't got a dragon,' she chortled. 'You're being silly, Uncle Kell.'

'We have mud, though,' Kell said sagely. 'Same thing. Mud eats people toe by toe. It's lucky you're wearing gum boots, Katie-bell, but our Beth is exposed at every single toenail.'

'But…are you going to rescue Beth, then?' the child demanded, fascinated.

'I sure am.' High on the bridge, Kell stripped off his disreputable shirt, eyed Beth with a wicked gleam and balanced himself on the wooden platform high above the river.

'You're coming down?' Katie squealed.

'Definitely,' Kell told her. 'I'm coming down in a flash almost worthy of Superman. And your job, Katie-bell, Rescuer's Accomplice Extraordinaire, is to prevent our maiden running away before I get there.'

'I don't think Beth can run,' Katie giggled, breathless with wonder at the silliness these two adults were engaged in. 'She's stuck in the mud up to her knees.'

'That's the very way I like my maidens best,' Kell approved, his voice bland as milk. 'Stuck.'

And without another word he curved his long body into a knifing dive—down, down into the deep, slow-moving currents of the river below.

Beth didn't run away. As Katie had said, she couldn't, but Beth couldn't have run even if the mud hadn't been holding her. She stood, staring with dumbstruck amazement down into the opaque water where Kell had disappeared.

Then, as the moments passed, she started to worry.

Surely Kell should have surfaced by now? How deep was the river? Was it safe to dive in here? Was the man crazy?

Beth stared out at the ever widening ripples round the place where Kell had entered the water and her breath caught in her throat. Kell… Kell…

She needn't have worried. He surfaced forty feet from the bridge—forty feet from where he'd entered the water and ten feet from where they were standing. His wicked smile hadn't faded one bit.

By her side, Katie squealed and squealed again in delight— and then backed behind Beth. As she hid she giggled, and her small body pressing against Beth's muddy legs shook with laughter. For the first time Beth knew the fear the child was showing wasn't real. Katie-bell was starting to believe that her Uncle Kell might just be fun.

Fun...

Was he fun? It was crazy to think that as Katie's nervousness of her uncle was fading Beth's was growing by the second.

There was ten feet of mud between Kell and the girls. The river must deepen quickly. Kell was only two feet from the river's edge now, but he appeared to be treading water, with only his head above the surface. He reached out with one hand, as if to take hold of the reeds growing along the edge. His hand slipped and he fell back.

'It's too deep here to get a foothold and it's muddy at the sides,' he complained, water streaming down over his dancing eyes. 'Beth, come and help. I need a hand to pull myself out.'

'You don't need anything,' Beth retorted breathlessly. 'You got yourself in there. You get yourself out.'

'You don't mean that?'

'Absolutely.' Beth stood firm—or rather she might have stood firm if the mud hadn't oozed traitorously downward.

'Damsels in distress are supposed to be co-operative,' Kell complained. 'It's in the union handbook.'

Beth's lips twitched, but she shook her head. She fought for a straight face—and she fought to stop her voice wobbling with something she couldn't define.

'Do you remember the nursery tale where the hero calls, "Rapunzel, Rapunzel, let down your hair"?' Beth managed. 'Do you know it, Katie-bell?' she asked the child at her side. She turned back to Kell. 'Every time I hear that tale, instead of thinking, How romantic! I think, Ouch! That's just the kind of girl I am, Mr Hallam—so maybe you'd better find yourself another maiden to rescue.'

'I'm not asking if I can pull myself out of the water using your hair as a tow rope,' Kell told her, wounded. 'I wouldn't. It's too darned pretty. All I want is a pull up with your hand, dear Beth, so I can climb onto the bank and transport my two ladies to a place of safety.' Then, as Beth folded her arms and looked immovable, he transferred his wounded gaze to his niece. 'Well, if Beth won't pull me from the water, how about you helping me, Katie-bell?'

'No way, Kell!' Beth frowned in swift concern. 'There's no way Katie's going near the edge.' She took the child's hand in hers again and gripped hard.

'But you won't help me, Beth,' Kell said sadly. He was a disembodied head floating on the surface of the water—a pair of wicked eyes with a challenging gleam.

'No. And Katie won't either.'

'You'll let me drown?'

'Yep!' Those dratted laughing eyes were doing something to Beth's insides that she didn't understand one bit.

'Katie, will you let your Uncle Kell stay here for ever, being eaten alive by the frogs and the water newts?' Kell called sadly. 'You wouldn't do that to your Uncle Kell, would you, Katie-bell?'

'Kell, don't you dare ask Katie to help.' Beth glanced down to find Katie's face creased in concern. 'That's not fair, Kell Hallam.'

'Katie could rescue me.'

'She mustn't...'

'Of course I'll help him,' Katie volunteered, and took a step forward. Beth pulled her back hard.

'Katie, you stay away from the water.'

'But, Beth, if you won't let me rescue my Uncle Kell, then you'll have to help him yourself,' Katie said urgently. 'The water's really, really deep. He'll drown.'

'Not him!'

'Beth, Katie's worried about me,' Kell called blandly. 'If you won't allow my niece to give me a hand, there's nothing for it, fair maiden, but to do your own rescue. And then I'll rescue you right back. I promise.'

'I didn't think maidens had to pre-pay their own rescue plan,' Beth said bitterly. She looked down at Katie's concerned face. The ground was being cut from under her—in more ways than one. Finally she took a tentative squelch forward. 'Katie, don't you move from there. And you, Kell Hallam... This is emotional blackmail.'

'I'm really good at it, aren't I?' Kell chuckled. 'There's no need to be so distrustful, my dear. My intentions are all innocent.'

'I'm starting to doubt you've ever had an innocent intention in your life,' Beth said bitterly—and then the memory of the night before swept over her in a rush that made her falter. Her colour mounted.

'Keep going,' Kell called encouragingly, as though he hadn't noticed her colour change—or her hesitation. 'I'm getting really tired of treading water.'

'Well, I'm getting really tired of squelching mud.'

'Go on, Beth,' Katie urged. 'Hurry up before he drowns.'

'He's a water rat,' Beth said dourly. 'Water rats don't drown.' But she took two more determined steps forward and finally reached dry land.

The very edge of the river was raised a little, forming a firm foothold where a few straggly water plants managed to exist. Behind Beth the river waters had broken to form the mud plain around them, but here at least she was safe from the all-enveloping mud. Safe—but coated in mud from shoulder to toe. And facing Kell Hallam.

'All you have to do is reach out,' Kell called encouragingly. His head was eighteen inches from her feet as he floated in the water. 'Just squat down and pull.'

'I don't know, Kell Hallam. I don't trust you,' Beth muttered softly. Who could trust those laughing eyes, mocking Beth from their watery vantage point?

'What on earth could I do to you?'

'Make me wet.'

'Would I?'

'Probably.'

'Oh, ye of little faith.' Kell smiled, his blandest and most beguiling smile. 'Dear Beth, just stoop and hold out your hand and you'll be rewarded amply.'

'How?'

'With something you really need.' Kell held out his hand imperatively. 'Enough talking. Save me before I drown.'

'Anyone less likely to drown...' Beth said crossly, but she stooped and held out her hand—and two seconds later she was falling into the water beside him, flying onto the river surface as the full force of Kell's hand pulled her forward.

Ten seconds later Beth surfaced in indignant fury, gasping for air. Kell had pulled her full length, so she'd gone under, but as soon as her body had sunk eighteen inches below the surface she'd met mud.

Kell was lying in the same shallow water. No wonder he'd called so confidently to Katie to help him! The man hadn't been putting the child in any danger. The water must be deep out where he'd dived, but here it was so shallow it must have been tricky for such a large male to keep up the impression he was treading deep water.

Beth opened her mouth to splutter her protest, spat out a mouthful of river water and tried again. 'You toad!' Her words came out as an indignant squeak.

She gasped with shock as she realised fully the trick that had been played on her, and, almost without thinking, she cupped her hands and sent a vast spray of muddy water out over the man before her. Then, for good measure, she twisted onto her back so her feet could kick up an even greater spray. For fully a minute there was nothing but water everywhere...nothing until Beth's indignation had burned itself out through sheer exhaustion and she fell back in the shallows in baffled silence.

Kell looked as if he'd hardly noticed the spray. As it ceased, however, he put a hand up to his sopping hair. 'Oh, Beth, you've wet me...' He sounded really sad.

It was too much. Beth gasped. She choked on laughter, bit it back, choked again, but then it bubbled out in a delicious rich sound that filled the morning air with delight.

'You...you...you absolute creep! Kell Hallam, you are a lying, deceiving weasel of a man and you should be ashamed of yourself!'

'Why should I be ashamed of myself?' Kell asked in innocence. 'I've done you a favour.'

'How have you done me a favour?' Beth was kneeling in the shallow water, her chestnut curls ribboning down over her shoulders in sodden strands and her T-shirt clinging wetly to her slim form. She should be wearing a bra, she thought in sudden panic, glancing down and then quickly up again before Kell noticed where she was glancing.

No such luck. Kell had certainly noticed. His eyes rested where she'd looked and the twinkle in his wicked eyes deepened.

'Well, firstly I've washed the mud off you.' He grinned. 'And secondly I'm seeing you in a whole new light.'

'So...how is that doing me a favour?' Beth's colour was fast mounting to a brilliant shade of rose. She sank so she was neck-deep in the water and her almost transparent T-shirt was hidden. 'S-seeing me, I mean?'

The laughter faded—just a little. 'I've a feeling you've been hiding your light under a bushel for far too long,' he said softly. There was a momentary pause and then the smile returned—gentler and more beguiling. 'Beth, I've been doing some hard thinking during the night.' He reached out under the water's surface and took her hand in his. 'Beth, if you won't come here as Katie's nanny, how about coming here as my wife?'

As a breathtaker it was a beauty. My wife... Beth stared blankly at the man before her and felt her jaw sag about six inches.

'P-pardon?'

'Beth, I'm asking you to marry me.'

Beth shook her head as though the water in her ears might be causing her difficulty in hearing. 'You... Kell, don't... Please... You must be crazy.'

'I'm not crazy, Beth. Why should I be crazy?'

For heaven's sake... It was as if he was offering her a cup of tea. Would you like this? Yes? No? One lump or two...?

Kell rose to his feet so he was thigh-deep in the shallow water and Beth was kneeling before him. He touched her streaming hair lightly with one finger as he watched the colour fade from her face. 'Don't look like that, Beth. It's a business proposition I'm offering you. A practical solution to both our needs—and you've assented once already to a marriage proposal like this. Surely my proposition can't be worse than Lyle's?'

Then, before Beth could answer, Kell turned his attention to the little girl staring at them agog from the riverbank. It was as if, having asked Beth his question, her answer wasn't of monumental importance.

Up on the bank Katie had been watching the two crazy adults with eyes enormous from shock. Kell's dogs had come rushing down from the bridge to be nearer their master and the child now had a dog standing sentinel at either side. The look on all their faces was the same. Dogs and child thought these two adult human persons cavorting in the river had lost their senses entirely.

They were right about at least one of the adults, Beth thought in disbelief as she struggled to find her footing in the shallows. She tried to stand—but Kell's hand fell on her shoulder and she was pushed firmly down again to kneeling.

'Stay in the water and have a proper swim, Beth,' he told her kindly. 'Would you like to come in too, Katie?' he called to his niece.

Katie stared at her uncle in open-mouth astonishment. Kell now had two females dumbfounded.

'It's wet in there,' Katie said slowly.

'The best water always is wet,' her uncle told her, his voice solemn. 'It's very good though. Isn't it, Beth?'

Beth opened her mouth like a fish—and shut it again. No words came out.

'Beth's having so much fun she can't describe it,' Kell informed his niece. He strode through the shallows, then out across the mud to where the little girl was standing. Maddeningly his feet hardly sank, even though, having discarded his boots before diving in, Kell was as barefoot as Beth had been. The dogs wriggled in delight as he approached, but Katie wasn't too sure.

Despite the shock of Kell Hallam's weird proposal, Beth found her attention focusing back on the child on the bank. Beth held her breath as Kell held out his arms to his niece.

'It's great in the water, Katie. Would you like to come in and play with me and Beth?'

Katie looked fearfully up at him.

'I've got my pinafore on.'

'So you have,' Kell agreed gravely. 'And we can't get your pinafore wet. But we could take it off and tuck it inside your gumboots. You could swim in just your knickers. Then your pinafore wouldn't even get wet.'

'You've wet all Beth's clothes,' Katie said accusingly, and Kell grinned.

'Well, yes. But Beth's clothes aren't nearly as important as your pinafore. Did you see, our Beth even has a hole in one knee of her jeans? Downright disgraceful, I'd say. We'll buy her some new ones when she comes to live with us.'

Beth gasped—and so did Katie.

'Is Beth coming to live with us?' Katie demanded.

'If we can persuade her. I think you should help me. Maybe she won't come to live with us yet—but if we try really, really hard we might convince her to come eventually. Now, Katie, our Beth is sitting all alone in the water, just aching for someone to play with. What about coming for a paddle with your Uncle Kell?' And he held his hand out in appeal.

There was a long, long moment of silence. Katie looked from Kell to Beth and then to the dogs at her sides. Then she looked to Beth again.

And finally Katie's hand came out.

'You won't let me go under the water, will you?' she whispered.

'No fear.' Kell swept the child up in his arms in a triumphant swoop. 'No fear, Katie love. I look after my womenfolk really well. I just hope… Well, I just hope we can persuade our Beth that she'd like being looked after as well as I intend to look after you.'

Our Beth…

The two words kept ringing in Beth's head over and over during the next half-hour.

The game Kell organised and bullied them into playing was silliness in the extreme—placing their hands into the mud in the shallows, letting their bodies float behind them and conducting hand-walking races along the bank. It was a ridiculous game, won each time by a triumphant Katie—if you excluded the dogs, who cheated by using four feet. Katie won because she was so light she didn't sink into the mud and need to haul her fingers out of their oozing trap before taking the next hand-step.

At the end of half an hour all of them were helpless with laughter—but Beth's head was spinning like a crazy twister.

What on earth was Kell thinking of to throw her such a crazy proposition? Surely he couldn't think she'd take it seriously? It didn't make any sense at all.

'It does make sense,' Kell told Beth finally, guessing her thoughts as Katie abandoned the adults as not worthy of racing and started her own silly race with just the dogs.

Kell sat down on the riverbank, his long legs stretched out before him in the shallows and the sun gleaming on his bare, wet torso. Beth knelt a little further away in the water—as if afraid of coming nearer.

'What makes sense?' There was nothing Beth could think of to do but to pretend misunderstanding. 'I don't...'

'Don't be thick, Beth,' Kell said kindly. 'You know what I mean. I mean marrying me.'

Beth swallowed. 'Kell...you're not serious. You don't want to marry me.'

'I don't want to marry anyone,' he told her calmly. 'At least...not in the sense that most people want marriage. I don't want romantic attachment. My parents tore each other apart with the demands they made on each other—and I've tried first hand—' Then he stopped, biting off his words. 'I'm not about to buy into that,' he said curtly. 'But with you...

'Well, you've shown me already you can view marriage as a business proposition, and if we can do that... Beth, you could stay here in your own apartments—have your animals and your interests and be a friend and mother to Katie. The social welfare people would get off my back about my unsuitability as a parent—and I'll admit I'm getting tired of their constant inquisitions. It doesn't do Katie any good either—to be constantly grilled by them as to how happy she is here. With you as my wife, Katie would have you forever.'

'But...'

'Beth, you say if you stayed then it would break your heart to leave,' Kell said urgently. 'I thought about it for most of last night—and it makes sense. If you married me then you'd never need to leave. Katie would have real stability. As well, I'd have a hostess for the place—which I'll admit I've lacked. I'm starting an experimental stud and I'm having more and more overseas business people staying here. They bring their wives—and it's a pest not having a hostess to entertain them while I talk business. I need a wife—but a wife without strings. A wife who views me as financial security but nothing else.'

'Nothing else? You mean...a wife without the emotional attachments.'

'That's it in one,' he agreed gravely. His mouth curved into a hint of a persuasive smile. 'We'd draw ourselves up a contract that sets out exactly what we expect of each other, and we'd follow the contract to the letter. That's not to say we couldn't be friends, Beth. I'm sure we can, or I'd never have suggested this. But we'd be independent.'

'But last night...' Beth swallowed, trying to formulate words from the jumble of crazy thoughts tumbling over and over in her mind. 'Kell, you didn't treat me then as though we could be just friends.'

'No.' Kell shook his head and his smile faded. He looked searchingly at the girl before him. 'No, I didn't, Beth, and that...well, I think that was a mistake. You're a beautiful woman—more beautiful than most I've known—but if we were to agree to this idea... Beth, you've already said you find me attractive, and I certainly do you, and that means we can

be proud of each other as husband and wife—but I don't think
we should take it further than that. Not without risking....'

'Risking me falling in love with you?' The question was a
whisper across the still morning air. Katie and the dogs were
checking a yabby hole further along the bank, three noses all
deep in mud. There was only Beth and Kell...man and
woman...with two yards of water between them. Two yards
of water that might as well be two miles.

'Beth, surely you wouldn't...?'

'I might,' Beth said miserably. 'And then...where would
that leave me? You don't want that sort of entanglement.
You've told me that very clearly. And Kell... Kell, I don't
think I could marry you without considering that as a possibility—any more than I could care for Katie as a business
proposition and then walk away. I'm not...'

'Not that level-headed?' Kell asked curiously. 'But you
were when your cousin propositioned you.'

'Well, there was never any fear of me falling head over
heels in love with Lyle,' Beth said shortly. She stood abruptly
up in the water and crossed her arms before her breasts in a
futile gesture of defence. 'Mr Hallam, I need to go home,
please. I'd like...I need you to take me home.'

'Beth, you aren't seriously saying you won't marry because
you might fall in love with me? That's ridiculous. It's romantic
nonsense that has no place in the real world.' Kell spread his
hands. 'Beth, in you I see a lovely girl with a huge heart
capable of so much caring. I see a woman I'd be proud to call
my wife. I can give you a good home, financial security and
a base for all your stray animals. Now and forever, Beth.
Think carefully before you throw it away.'

'I've already thought,' Beth said miserably, staring down at
the muddied water around her feet. 'Kell...Mr Hallam,
please...please take me home.'

'You mean back to the house?'

'No,' Beth said bleakly. 'I mean back to my home, please, Kell Hallam. Back to where I belong. Back to where I'm by myself again.'

CHAPTER EIGHT

THE hours it took to cover the drive southwards to Beth's farm were dreadful.

Katie sat in the rear seat, quiet as the little possum hanging back around Beth's neck. Kell made desultory small talk, but even he gave up in the face of Beth's inability to answer in anything but monosyllables.

She had taken a shower and changed her clothes before the drive. She was physically comfortable—but inwardly anything but! She saw the turn-off to her farm with real relief. Any more time with this man and she was starting to think she'd go crazy.

In comparison with Kell Hallam's luxurious home, Beth's looked almost ridiculous. Her land was marginal coastal farmland, set at the edge of national forest with the bush always threatening to reclaim its own. The farmhouse was a tiny weatherboard cottage, dwarfed by the huge gums around it and by the bushland that was reclaiming the house yard. Years of neglect by absentee landlords had meant the cottage was ramshackle to the point of being derelict. Only Beth's love over the last few years had managed to hold it together, but that wouldn't be the case for much longer.

It didn't need to hold together for much longer, Beth thought sadly as they pulled to a halt in front of the house. She had no money now to pay for the lease. Within a month she'd be walking away from this place.

To where? Who knew? The only thing Beth knew for sure was that she would be walking alone.

Katie was cautiously climbing from the car, her eyes wide as saucers as she took in the place before her.

'It's pretty, Beth,' she said cautiously. 'But...it's really, really old.'

'It is.' Beth made a huge effort and managed a smile as she joined Katie. Kell emerged from the driver's seat as well and looked round in silence. Beth cast a doubtful glance at him, trying to read his expression, but gave it up as a bad job. Who knew what this man was thinking?

'This is a real Australian farmhouse, Katie,' she managed, trying hard to focus her attention only on the child. 'Not like your uncle's squatter's homestead. Your uncle has toilets that flush with water and connect to sewerage systems. Here we have a real Australian dunny! Want to see?'

'Uncle Kell has dunnies,' Katie retorted obstinately, but Beth shook her head.

'No.' Beth glanced again at Kell—then as quickly glanced away again. 'No real, self-respecting dunny lives inside the house. No proper dunny has flushing water. My dunny has a proper pan underneath. In short, it's the genuine article.'

'A pan? What do you mean, a pan?'

Beth grinned and held out her hand, pointing to the tiny outhouse beside her cottage.

'Let's introduce you to a real Aussie dunny, Katie-bell. See how it leans over? I was in it one night in a storm and the whole thing blew over. Only the seat and the can were left standing. It looked ridiculous—and I looked even more ridiculous, sitting on a seat with no little house around me. Now I've had to tie my little outhouse down with steel ropes. Let's look at my dunny, then I'll ring Caroline—she's the girl who cares for my animals while I'm away—and tell her I'm home so she doesn't need to do the evening feed, and after that I'll introduce you to all my creatures.'

It was a strange tour. Katie was avidly interested, watching Beth closely as she checked the well-being of each of her charges. But at the same time the child clutched Beth, as if afraid that any minute she would disappear into thin air.

And Kell... Kell followed them silently behind, a long, lean and silent presence. The man hardly spoke—but Beth knew he was taking everything in with his direct, intelligent eyes. He was seeing Beth's near-derelict house. He was seeing her kitchen, with its jars and bottles of herbs and ointments and her orphan pouches hanging from chairs. He was seeing her animals. But he was watching her...

Beth was showing Kell and Katie some quite amazing animals. Katie's distress at her imminent loss of Beth gradually faded in the presence of the stray creatures. The child was introduced to one after the other and for each she demanded to be told a full life history. What had happened to the little koala's mother? How had the kangaroo in the back paddock been injured? Why did the little echidna lap milk from Beth's hand rather than from a bottle?

Katie's questions were intelligent beyond her years, and Beth found herself wondering at the child's months of self-enforced silence. With this intelligent little tongue at rest since her mother died, all Katie had done was think and listen, and her knowledge was astounding.

'Mummy used to tell me all about Australian animals,' Katie told Beth proudly at the end of the tour. Then she tentatively turned to her uncle. 'Uncle Kell, if Beth can't stay with us any more, why can't we stay with Beth for a while. It'd be like...like a holiday. We could help Beth look after her babies.' She took a deep breath, as if offering the supreme sacrifice. 'And I'll even use Beth's dunny!'

'Greater love hath no child!' Her uncle smiled. He took his niece's hand and looked gravely at Beth. For the first time since they'd arrived he spoke to her directly. 'Beth, Katie's idea is good. It's after four already and it's a three-hour drive home. How do you feel about putting us up for the night?'

'But I haven't...'

'You don't have accommodation?' They were standing in Beth's little kitchen, and Kell's large presence almost filled it. To one side lay her tiny bedroom, and the parlour was the only other room—a rather odd parlour, given over to animal comforts rather than human comforts, but inviting for all that.

'I can see you're stretched.' Kell smiled, and his dark eyes twinkled. 'The orphans take precedence in this place. But I did have the forethought to pack air mattresses and sleeping bags. Katie and I will sleep on the verandah. It'll be an adventure, if you like. Will you have us?'

Beth stared. Would she have this man stay here? Here in her sanctuary? 'But...there's no food in the house,' she faltered.

'So what were you planning to eat tonight?'

'There's...I guess there'll be eggs in the chook run...and I'll milk Daisy.'

'Daisy?'

'She's my one remaining goat,' Beth said sadly. 'Daisy was in the hayshed in labour when the dogs killed the rest of the herd. Her milk's lovely...but you two can't have a meal of just eggs and milk.'

'Of course we can,' Katie said solidly from her uncle's side. 'Eggs and milk is my favourite dinner. It's your favourite too, isn't it, Uncle Kell?'

'Only if the company is good.' Kell smiled again, his expression growing thoughtful. 'And I have to say that the company here seems to be excellent. If you'll have us, Miss Beth Lister, my niece and myself would love to accept your gracious invitation to dine and spend the night in your wonderful home. Just show us which part of the verandah is the softest.'

'Really?'

'Really.'

'Well, okay,' Beth managed dubiously. She eyed Kell as one would eye a coiled snake. 'As long as you definitely do sleep on the verandah.' She relented a little as she looked down at Katie. 'Kate-bell can share my bed if she likes—but strange men have to stay outside after dark.'

'Uncle Kell's not strange,' Kate objected.

'He's strange enough.' Beth glared at Kell. He was definitely strange enough to sleep on the back verandah. Beth was just wondering whether her verandah was far enough away. She really didn't want this man anywhere near her.

Still... Beth's glare softened as an idea took root. Kell Hallam was one very large male. And very large males had their uses. If he was going to stay...

'Well, there's a cost if you really do want to stay,' Beth told him slowly, a plan forming in her head as she spoke. She'd needed someone like Kell Hallam for a long time now. If he was here... If he was definitely staying... 'This five-star resort accommodation comes with a hefty price tag,' she told him. 'My verandah is very, very expensive.'

'Uncle Kell has lots of money,' Katie pronounced, and then looked dubiously up at her uncle. 'Haven't you, Uncle Kell?'

'I might,' Kell told his niece. His face was still—his dark eyes still perusing Beth's with a thoughtful expression. 'But then again...I get the feeling, Katie-bell, that our Beth might not be talking money here. Now, why do I feel that? And am I right?'

'You sure are.' Despite her misgivings, Beth's smile dimpled out. She smiled down to Kate. 'Your accommodation is free because you're six, Katie-bell, and six years old isn't old enough to pay. But your uncle Kell...'

'Yes?' Kell was smiling too, but his face continued to show a trace of doubt and Beth's smile grew accordingly. It was nice to throw this man off balance for a change. Heaven knew, he'd thrown Beth's equilibrium off balance enough.

'All my wood's green,' she told him demurely.

'Pardon?'

'My wood,' Beth said again, as if her explanation was obvious. 'I've been cutting firewood from gums fallen on the property but I'm out of old timber. However...'

'However?' Kell repeated her word with foreboding.

'However—' Beth dimpled again and winked down at Katie '—there's a vast old red gum in the far paddock, and it's been dead for years. Every storm I wonder if it'll fall and every storm it doesn't. It's too dangerous to climb high enough to lop its branches one by one, but if it fell... If it fell the right way I'd have enough wood to last for years. Or at least...' Her voice faltered.

'At least you'd have enough wood to last until you moved from here,' Kell finished for her, unerringly interpreting the wave of unhappiness behind Beth's pause. He frowned. 'So...I gather you'd just like me to wander out and fell this giant before tea as part of our accommodation package. Is that it?'

'Got it in one.' Beth shook aside her momentary sadness and beamed. 'Is that okay?'

'Beth...'

'Mr Hallam, I'll help you,' Beth assured him blithely. 'In fact, I usually fell all my own timber. But *this* one... It's sited near the dam on a piece of land that juts out into the water, and if it falls the wrong way it'll end up under the surface. If it does that, then it's useless for anything other than yabby habitat. My yabbies seem contented enough without it, so I really don't want it falling in the water.'

'Or on you.'

'It won't fall on me. I'm not that stupid,' Beth assured him. 'I know how to fell a tree. But this one's branches are lopsided, and if it falls even slightly sideways I'm in trouble. Want to see?'

'No,' Kell said definitely and with feeling. 'I don't.'

'No tree, no accommodation. Not even any goat's milk,' Beth said firmly, only a faint twinkle behind her eyes belying her innocent expression. 'That's the deal.'

'And what about Katie?' Kell said in exasperation. 'Are you proposing the three of us set out on a tree-felling expedition?'

'I told you—Katie's accommodation is free,' Beth assured him. She crouched down beside Katie. 'Katie-bell, if you want to stay here, then your uncle Kell has a job to do. I want him to help chop down a tree. Now, you can see the tree from the verandah. What if I take you out to where my little wallabies are eating fuchsias under my bedroom window? You can look after them and watch what we're doing at the same time. Will you do that?'

'I might,' Katie said cautiously. 'I'd rather help chop down a tree.'

'I know you would,' Beth smiled. 'But six is a bit young to hold a chainsaw and my wallabies need a babysitter. If you promise to stay here and not move from the verandah, then your uncle and you will stay here for the night. How about that?'

'That's blackmail,' Kell said sharply, and Beth gave him her sweetest smile.

'Two can play at that game, then—can't they, Mr Hallam? I seem to remember you using your niece to entice me into the water this morning. Now, if you'll just wait until I feed my possum and fetch some fuchsias for my wallabies, then we'll go and chop down one gum tree.'

'You have to be kidding!'

Ten minutes later Beth and Kell were standing at the base of one of the biggest red gums on the property. The tree towered over them—its long-dead branches forming an eerie canopy between the ground and the sinking sun. The shadow over the grass was of a huge skeleton of some long-dead creature—beautiful and yet infinitely sad.

'No, I'm not kidding,' Beth said softly. She looked up into the leafless branches and her face grew sad. 'It's had its life. The trunk really is rotten. It will come down all on its own if we don't cut it, and even if I'm not here to use the timber someone else will be. It's too good to let it fall underwater.'

'Well, you're not cutting it,' Kell retorted, watching the changing expressions flit over Beth's face. His own eyes betrayed little. They'd come over to the dam on the tractor that Beth leased with the farm—an enormous Massey Ferguson that looked older than Beth. Beth had sat on the driver's seat while Kell stood beside her on the step. She had put her chainsaw—almost as elderly as her tractor—onto the tractor tray, along with a couple of hard hats. Now Kell looked behind and grimaced at the hats. 'What help are they going to be?' he demanded.

'Well, they might mark the spot where we go under if the tree falls on us.' Beth grinned. 'The ground around the dam is nice and soft. We'd save burial fees—and the helmets would make a good marker.'

'Don't be facetious.' Despite his retort Kell couldn't quite suppress an answering smile. 'Look, Beth, you can't really be intending to cut this tree. It's a job for trained men—not a slip of a girl.'

'I've cut trees as big as this by myself before,' Beth assured him. 'It's wonderful what you can do when you don't have the money to call on a team of men. If you're frightened, though...'

'I'm not bloody frightened!' Kell's brow snapped down. 'Look, if it really needs to come down, then I'll send a few of my men down here to help.'

'I don't need your men.' Beth switched off the tractor engine and slid from the seat. She stood on the far side of the tractor and glared at him. 'I can do this. All I need is for you to attach the tractor to the cable, take up the slack and then, when the tree starts moving, give it a tug in the right direction.'

'Do you have any idea what would happen if it fell in the wrong direction?' Kell demanded incredulously, and Beth nodded.

'Of course I do.' Beth placed her hands on her denim-clad hips and glared. 'First of all I'd be squashed, because I'd be standing behind it—and secondly, if you were on an attached tractor and the tree fell backwards, then you'd probably end up flying backwards too, at a rate of knots so fast you wouldn't know what hit you. But that won't happen.'

'Why not?'

'Because I know how to fell trees,' Beth said in exasperation. 'Mr Hallam, the only reason I need help with this one is that it has to fall straight out. I'm sure I can get it to fall in the rough direction I want—I've felled trees heaps of times and I do know what I'm doing—but here…even if it falls a little sideways then it'll go under water and I'll lose at least some of it. I can't scuba dive to chop firewood, so I'm forced to ask for help. Now, will you help me or not?'

'This is ridiculous.' Kell shook his head. He gazed out over the paddocks. 'Beth, there are at least three other dead trees in view. They must be as good as this—and not so precariously placed. I'll fell one of them for you.'

'No,' Beth said stubbornly. 'There are six dead trees on the property, but none as rotten as this and the others are all good habitat trees. There are parrots nesting in the trunks, and possums, and all sorts of creatures making their homes in them. I won't cut them down. If I have to leave here then the next tenants will need firewood, and they might think it easier to cut down the habitat trees if this isn't already felled. So... It has to be this one.'

Kell shook his head, as if clearing a fog. 'Beth, you're not going to do this.'

'I am,' Beth said softly. 'Whether you help me or not. I'm all set up. I've just been waiting for someone to come...' Her voice faltered and she looked swiftly away from Kell. It sounded pathetic. Those words. She'd just been waiting for someone...

'Your cousin Lyle came.'

Beth studiously studied her toes. They were now respectably clad in leather working boots—much better than the scanty footwear she'd been forced to wear when at this man's home—but her feet still didn't feel right. Nothing about her felt right.

'Lyle doesn't help me,' she said in a small voice. 'He never has.'

'You really don't like him, do you?' Kell asked intently, watching Beth's face as she stared at the ground. And then his voice changed. 'You're afraid of him. Physically?'

'No-no. Not now.'

'He's hurt you in the past?'

Beth shook her head, as though ridding herself of a bad dream. 'Kell, please...I don't want to remember.'

Silence.

'So...who will help if I don't?' Kell asked at last, frowning, as if he suspected her of some trickery.

'There's a farmer a couple of miles up the road—Caroline's dad,' Beth told him. 'Sometimes he uses me as cheap labour and then he'll give me a hand with jobs like this as payment.'

'You really are on your own, aren't you?' Kell said softly. There was another long silence—and then he shook his head. 'Beth, you must see that you can't do this, though. If anything happened...'

'Do you really think anything would happen?' Beth demanded, lifting her eyes to face him. 'Do you think I'd run that risk—to Katie as well as to us? Kell, you know what I'm asking isn't dangerous.'

'Not if you let me fell the tree,' Kell retorted. 'I know how to get it to fall right.'

'Are you saying I don't?'

'I'm saying I don't trust you.'

'Then the feeling's mutual.' Hands on her hips, Beth glared.

'Okay.' Kell threw up his hands in mock surrender. 'Okay, Miss Fire-eater. Let's say you're a tree-feller extraordinaire. Let's concede that. The tree's rotten, though, Beth, and you know we need to attach a cable to the top branches to hook up to the tractor. We need a cherry-picker to raise one of us high enough to do that.'

'No.' Beth shook her head. She ducked out from behind the tractor, dived behind the dead tree and hauled a thick metal cable out from where it had been hanging on the far side of the trunk. 'The cable's already been attached.'

Kell practically gaped.

'How the hell...?'

'I climbed,' Beth said kindly. 'You should shut your mouth. You'll catch flies if you don't.'

'You climbed...' In seemingly one swift movement Kell lunged round the tractor, round the tree to where Beth stood, and seized Beth's shoulders. His grip was like iron as he held the slip of a girl before him. 'You climbed the tree! Beth, do you have any idea...any idea at *all* how dangerous that was? You stupid little... Beth, you could have killed yourself!'

'I need the firewood, Mr Hallam,' Beth said simply. 'Without warmth my little creatures die. This is the only source of heat I can afford.'

'So you'd risk your life—'

'Not such a risk,' Beth told him gently, pulling away. His

hands, though, refused to release her. 'I didn't go out on any of the branches and I was up and down the tree so fast you'd think I was a possum myself. I had to be ready, you see... I had to be ready in case there was an opportunity like this one. And now...Kell... Mr Hallam, will you help me, please?'

Kell stared down at her. His hands still gripped and his face was incredulous as his eyes met hers.

'I've never...never...' he said slowly, and shook his head. His voice faded as though he couldn't find words to frame the thought.

'You've never helped a woman chop down a tree?' Beth put her hands up and lifted Kell's arms so that the hold on her shoulders was broken. 'Shame on you, Mr Hallam,' she managed, striving for lightness. 'Shame. Put on your hard hat, then, in case of falling twigs, and let's get on with it. There's a first time for everything.'

Kell wouldn't let Beth touch the chainsaw.

'I know how to do this,' she expostulated, but he refused even to listen.

'You drive the tractor,' he told her grimly. 'At least this way I know it'll be done right.'

'But—'

'No buts, Beth Lister,' he ordered. 'You want help? You accept help on my terms—so shut up and watch. We'll hook the cable to the tractor first and get it far enough away so the tree can't possibly fall on it—and then your job for the time being is just to watch.'

So there was nothing for Beth to do in the short term but just that—shut up and watch.

To her considerable relief, Kell did know how to handle a chainsaw.

Not that she had expected anything else, Beth thought to herself as she watched Kell expertly cut a scarf—a neat wedge a third of the thickness of the tree trunk—from the landward side of the tree. The scarf meant the tree must fall in the direction of the wedge as soon as the chainsaw was applied to the far side of the trunk.

Kell was good. Beth had to admit that as she watched him size up the tree, taking note of the differing weightings of the sideways branches and cutting his scarf accordingly. The wedge he cut was as good as—or, if she was honest, even better than—any Beth could have cut herself.

She watched in silence—there was little else she could do above the roar of the chainsaw—and when the scarf came free she stood back and waited while Kell checked his work and looked up into the dead branches.

'It's as good as we'll get,' Kell told her. 'But you're right. We still need the weight of the tractor to pull it where we want it to go. Beth...'

'Now, don't go having any more qualms,' she told him severely, keeping her own nervousness in check. 'You know the wedge is good. I'm only pulling the tree round by five degrees or less as it falls—and that means even if I don't succeed in pulling it the tractor will only skid a few feet.' She gave Kell a cheeky smile. 'You've done almost as well as I could have.'

Then, without waiting for Kell's startled retort, she turned to where the tractor was extending the cable past the far reaches of the tree's likely path. Beyond the tractor in the next paddock she could see the house—and Katie still happily playing on the verandah. 'All personnel accounted for,' she told Kell lightly. 'Sure you don't want me to cut?'

'I don't want you to do anything,' Kell said bluntly, catching his breath. 'Except leave this to someone else.'

'If I were another man, would you have such doubts?' Beth asked curiously, and watched his face.

She'd touched a nerve. His eyes widened—and Kell gave

himself a visible shake. A faint smile started at the back of his eyes.

'Are you accusing me of being a chauvinist, Miss Lister?' Kell demanded. 'Is that what you think I am?'

'I'm sure all the best men are,' Beth said enigmatically. 'At least—all the men who *think* they're the best. Now, shall we get on with the job, Mr Hallam, or shall we have a discussion on political correctness right here and now?' Her green eyes twinkled. 'I warn you, I'm bound to win any debate on feminine superiority.'

'How do you figure that?'

'Women's intuition.' She grinned. 'And the fact that I'm on the tractor and you're on the chainsaw, Mr Hallam. The sex with the biggest instrument is always right. Isn't that so?' And with a last twinkle she ran lightly back over to the tractor and started it up. 'Okay, Mr Hallam,' she called over the noise of the Massey Ferguson. 'Over to you. And just remember—if we mess this up, they'll write "We deserved it" on our hard hats.'

'Gee, thanks, Miss Lister,' Kell called back, revving his chainsaw into action and raising his voice to match. 'Your confidence in the pair of us is underwhelming!'

And two minutes later the vast gum came crashing down.

The crack as Kell's chainsaw bit deep enough to make the dead giant topple sounded like a volley of rifles. At the sound Beth shoved her foot on the accelerator, the tractor heaved forward—and the giant tree fell exactly where Beth wanted it.

The entire tree was on dry land.

It took minutes for the vast skeleton to settle—branches quivering into stillness where they lay. Beth stopped the tractor, then looked anxiously back. Kell was at the stump—looking just as anxiously out at her.

All safe. All done.

Beth climbed from the tractor and looked out over the fallen branches and vast trunk—and to her dismay she felt tears welling at the back of her eyes.

It looked so dead. So…so final. The tree had been a thing of beauty for hundreds of years, and now its life was over.

Even so… Beth had wanted this tree down for months. She'd needed this wood so badly. And now… This tree would keep her in fuel for two years or more—but she didn't have two years left.

She didn't have two months.

Some new owner would come and use this giant. Her giant. The tree she and Kell had felled.

Beth shoved a hand up to wipe away tears, furious with herself for showing so much weakness. How could she be so weak as to cry now? To cry for a dead tree—and a future she didn't have?

And then Kell was suddenly beside her, his arms coming round her and pulling roughly in to lie against his body. It was as if he'd expected this reaction. Expected her sadness.

'No need to cry, Beth,' he said softly. There was the trace of a smile in his voice. 'I wasn't squashed. I wasn't even close to being squashed.'

'I didn't think…' Beth made a futile effort to pull away, but that was all it was—futile. 'I'm not crying because of you. I didn't think you'd be squashed.'

'So why are you crying?'

Kell's hands came up and pressed her face into his shoulder. For a long moment Beth resisted—but then the need for comfort became almost unbearable. She buried her head in the thick, masculine feel of his shirt and let his hand stroke her hair as it willed. As he willed.

'I'm not…' Beth choked. 'I only cry…because it's dead.'

'It died a long time ago,' Kell said gravely. He wasn't laughing at her. In some strange way he seemed to understand.

'You'll have to find some better excuse than that to cry. It wouldn't be that you're crying because you're leaving this place, would it, Beth?'

'No.' With a gasp Beth managed to pull away, shoving a grimy fist over her tearstained cheeks. She stepped back from him and glared. 'No. Anyway...that's not your business, Kell Hallam.'

'It is my business,' he said gravely. 'You'd figured out a way to save your farm—to save your livelihood. If you'd married Lyle then you wouldn't have to leave here, and I've interfered with that. You have to let me make amends.' He took a step forward and held her shoulders. 'Beth, if you won't marry me then let me buy this place for you. It was going to be a marriage settlement from Lyle. Now...let it be a non-marriage settlement from me.'

'No!' Beth shook her head. She pulled back from his arms but his hands brooked no challenge. 'Kell, no...'

'Why not?'

'Because I won't be—be indebted to you,' she stammered. 'I won't. I'm managing on my own. I don't want you to have any hold on me. I'll manage on my own—or not at all.'

'"Not at all" sounds pretty bleak,' Kell said gently, and his dark eyes searched hers with understanding. 'Beth, it'll break your heart to leave your animals. I haven't known you long—but I've known you long enough to know that. Beth, you have to let me help.'

'I don't *have* to do anything.' She hauled herself from him then, and took two hasty steps back as he made to follow. 'No.' She shook her head. 'Kell...Lyle had no business promising me what he did. He was cheating Katie—depriving her of what's hers. Somehow he conned me into his plans, but just because I was stupid enough to be conned doesn't mean that you have to pay.'

'I want to pay.'

'No, you don't,' she said miserably. 'No, you—'

'How do you know what I want?'

'Kell Hallam, until yesterday you hadn't even met me,' she told him. 'I refuse to take money from you because you feel sorry for me. I just won't. So stop talking about it and… and…'

She looked up despairingly—and then round to stare at the house, where Katie was patiently standing on the verandah. Even from here it was clear the child was aching to rejoin the adults. 'Please…Katie's been by herself for too long,' she told him. 'If you could walk back to Katie and keep her company—I'll chop enough wood for tonight's cooking.'

'I'll chop the wood.' Kell's eyes didn't leave her. 'Beth, let me…'

Beth shook her head. 'No.' Her voice was bleak but hard. 'I don't want any more help from you, Mr Hallam. You've done enough. You've given me enough firewood to last me all the time I have left in this place. That's your debt paid in full, Mr Hallam. And now…now I want to be left alone. I'll chop enough wood for tonight and bring it back on the tractor and I'll do it alone. That's the way it has to be, Mr Hallam. I've been alone all my life—and I don't intend to lose my independence now.'

And Beth turned and walked away to where she'd left the chainsaw—and she didn't look back.

Kell Hallam was left staring after her—and the expression on his face was totally unreadable.

CHAPTER NINE

SOMEWHAT to Beth's surprise, Kell did leave her. She was left to saw her wood by herself while he walked back over the paddocks to rejoin his niece.

It was comforting in a way—to be left with such a task. To be left with a job that took concentration, that took her thoughts from Kell's unsettling, unnerving presence. Beth revved up the chainsaw again and didn't stop cutting until she'd stacked almost a ton of stove-sized timber. Then she loaded the small tray of the tractor and made her way back home.

Back to where Katie—and Kell—were waiting.

Beth had left returning until she had no choice. The sun had set half an hour ago. Only the faint glow of dusky pink over the mountains echoed the sun enough to guide her path.

Katie and Kell were settled on the verandah, patiently waiting, just as Beth had expected. To her surprise, though, there was a wisp of smoke trailing up out of the cottage chimney—smoke faintly perceptible in the night sky but made more obvious by the sweet scent of burning eucalypt. Nestled in the surrounding bushland, the cottage looked beautiful in the fading light and Beth felt a lump settle hard in her throat.

This was her home. For the weeks since Lyle had thrown his marriage proposal at her, Beth had allowed herself to hope that she could stay. Now there was no such reprieve.

And the picture of man and child nestled on the verandah didn't help the lump in her throat one bit. Kell Hallam...

Beth parked her tractor below the verandah and looked up at her self-invited guests. The porch light was on, casting a

soft light across man and child. Kell had found the only comfortable armchair in the place and dragged it outside. He was
now installed on its deep cushions, with his niece sleepily
cradled in his arms. They looked a picture—this farmer or
kidnapper or photographer with his orphaned niece in his
arms—and Beth found her heart twist even further. They
looked… They looked like father and child… This domestic
scene was so…so…

So darned dangerous. So deceptive. This man might sit here
looking as if he belonged to her home, but Kell had no place
here. No place in her life.

'What have you used to light my fire?' Beth asked, fighting
emotion and summoning suspicion to take its place.

'You sound as if you reckon I've been ripping up your
floorboards for firewood.' Kell's voice was lazy and slow. He
smiled down at the girl on the tractor. 'Distrustful woman!
No, Bethany, we haven't touched your precious floorboards—
though some of them look like they're better suited for firewood than they are for flooring. Katie and I went on a foraging
expedition. We found enough twigs and loose leaves to light
a small fire—though your contribution will still be very nice,
of course.' Kell ended on a magnanimous note that made
Beth's pain recede a little and the sides of her mouth twitch
into an involuntary smile.

'Gee, thanks.' Beth swung herself down from the tractor
and walked slowly up to join them. Katie-bell looked up from
Kell's arms, gave Beth a sleepy smile and nestled closer into
Kell's arms. Beth saw the snuggle with soft satisfaction.
Things were changing here fast. A relationship was forming
between Katie and her uncle almost before Beth's eyes.

It was as if Katie had withheld her trust for so long she
could bear the isolation no longer. The little girl's silence had
been her barrier, and the barrier was now down. Here were
her adults, the child's sleepy smile said. This was her home.

Only Beth wasn't her adult. Beth's home wasn't Katie's home.

More heart lurching. Beth fought back a sudden pricking behind her eyes. Damn this man. Damn this situation that was tearing at her heartstrings in a way that had never happened in her life before.

'I should have been back before this,' she faltered. 'Katie will be hungry.'

'Katie's not hungry,' Kell told her. 'We're a very resourceful couple, Katie-bell and I. We've initiated an egg hunt and found twenty! And we've milked your goat. Katie's had two boiled eggs and some toast soldiers. We did find some bread in your freezer—but there's not a lot else in there. You really do live rough, Miss Lister.'

'You milked Daisy?' Beth managed, not listening to anything after this startling revelation. 'How on earth…?'

'With great difficulty,' Kell admitted. 'She's some goat.'

'Your nasty goat kicked my Uncle Kell,' Katie's sleepy voice declared from her Uncle Kell's arms. 'Twice. And she tried to bite him, but Uncle Kell called her a—'

'Katie-bell, never you mind what your Uncle Kell called her,' Kell said hastily. 'You can just forget you heard that, young lady. What matters is that we succeeded—and Katie-bell's had her dinner. We've even found some fresh fuchsias for your two wallabies—they appeared to be right out of supplies by the look of the bare twigs on the verandah, and one of them came right into the kitchen and made his displeasure known as if he was boss of the place. But now… Now if our landlady, Beth, can pop one Katie-bell into bed, I think it's time she settled down to sleep—and then I'll cook tea for the landlady.'

'Will you make toast soldiers for Beth like you did for me?' Katie asked, settling back to sleepiness as Kell rose with his small burden.

'I'll make an omelette for Beth,' Kell said firmly, kissing his niece on her nose. 'Toast soldiers are for special girls.'

'But Beth's special.'

'So she is.' Kell's voice softened. He glanced across at Beth—and then swiftly back to Katie-bell. 'So she is. Even if she does own some very peculiar animals. You're very right to remind me, Katie-bell. Bethany may have a toast soldier if she requires one. Or even two. Now, Beth, if you'll help me put this scamp to bed, I'll get started in the kitchen.'

'But...I'll cook,' Beth managed, thoroughly unsettled. 'Kell, you're not cooking...'

'Oh, yes, I am,' Kell retorted strongly. 'My chauvinist father always made the delineation of the sex roles quite clear. One sex hunts, chops wood and does the rough stuff. The other sex cooks, cleans and does the householding. My father must have had his sexes mixed—or maybe you have, Bethany Lister— but I know what's what, Miss Hunter-Gatherer. You chopped our wood, so I'm cooking. So shut up and enjoy it. Right?'

'R-right.'

Only it didn't seem right at all. It felt stranger than any sensation Beth had ever experienced in her life.

It only grew stranger.

With Katie sleeping peacefully in Beth's big bed, she and Kell had the house to themselves—orphaned animals ex- cepted. To Beth's surprise her omelette was already half pre- pared—eggs separated, herbs chopped at the ready and her biggest pan heating to red-hot on the wood stove. To her fur- ther surprise a bottle of white wine stood opened on the table.

'This isn't mine,' Beth said cautiously, lifting the bottle of Chardonnay and inspecting it rather as one would inspect an ants' nest. 'Where did you find it?'

'I brought it with me, of course,' Kell told her blandly. 'I

always come prepared. Would you like to change for dinner?'
He looked pointedly down at Beth's stained jeans.

'Why?' Beth sat down heavily on a kitchen chair and glared.
Wine, for heaven's sake… And changing for dinner… What
was he suggesting? That she slip on an evening dress? She bit
her lip and shook her head. 'I've washed my hands,' she said,
a trace of defiance in her voice. 'What more do you want?'

Kell blinked—and then grinned. 'I've met women who
spend hours on their evening toilette.' Kell's tone was distinctly approving. He lifted the egg whisk in a mock salute.
'And you…you wash your hands and sit down at the table—
ready for the meal of a lifetime.'

'The meal of a lifetime… You don't half have a high opin-
ion of your own ability,' Beth snapped, thoroughly unnerved.
'I'd rather not have any wine, thank you.'

'Why not?'

'Because…'

'Because you don't trust yourself?' Kell smiled down at the
girl before him, and his smile was a caress all in itself. It took
Beth's remaining breath right away. 'Beth, have you so little
trust in me? I swear I won't seduce you.'

'I know…'

'You don't look as though you know.' Kell's smile deepened as he started to whisk his eggs. 'Beth, you have to believe
you're safe. Apart from your own very effective anti-seduction
glare, your verandah is rock-hard and liberally sprinkled with
wallaby droppings. There's no room in your bed for me along
with Katie-bell and assorted orphaned animals, your back-
yard's so overgrown I'd need a machete to clear a love-nest,
and the ground in front of your verandah has prickles. I
checked. So… A wise man knows when he's beaten—and I
know when I'm beaten.'

'But… Are you ever beaten?' Beth whispered. 'I expect
your line of seduction works very nicely.'

Kell's hand stilled. The eggs lay half whisked and now ignored. 'Beth, what do you think I am?' Kell asked curiously. 'I have the feeling you think me some sort of womaniser.'

'I never said that.'

'You implied it.'

'Well...' Beth stared at the scrubbed wooden surface of her table and refused to meet his eyes. 'I guess... You're rich and attractive...and you've made it clear that you don't want marriage except as a matter of convenience. I suppose... Well, you're not gay...'

'No, Beth, I'm not gay.' Kell bent over the table and his hand caught her chin, forcing her eyes up to his. 'Did you think I might be?'

'No,' Beth whispered. 'I know you're not. But... I mean, when you kissed me...'

'You assumed I kiss any attractive woman who crosses my path?' He nodded and released her, and he started to whisk again. 'I suppose I deserve that. But, no, Beth, I don't seduce lightly. I kissed you because I found you altogether too desirable for words—but I put that desire away almost as soon as I felt it. I've learned the hard way that you don't make life decisions when you're being controlled by emotions.'

'I'm not a life decision,' Beth whispered, and Kell's hand stilled again.

'No. I suppose you're not now,' he said softly. 'When I asked you to marry me—well, that was a common sense request...'

'It wasn't in the least common sense.'

'For me it was,' Kell corrected her. 'I also believe it was for you—but you don't see it like that. You haven't learned to separate head and heart, Beth Lister. It's a hard lesson.'

'But you've learned it.'

'Yes, I've learned it,' Kell admitted, his voice flat and definite. 'Everybody does in the end. And it always seems to me that the longer it takes to learn the lesson, the harder the blow at the end. So...'

'So?'

Kell sighed. 'So shut up and let me make you an omelette, Beth. Let's ignore both heads and hearts and concentrate on really important issues.'

'Such as?'

'Such as our stomachs.' He smiled, as though pushing unwanted thoughts aside. 'And have a glass of wine, beautiful Bethany. Even *your* head must tell you there's no danger in one glass.'

Maybe not. Beth looked up at the man before her and knew that danger was all around her. Danger...

Danger of falling so deeply in love that she'd never escape its heart-pull. Danger that her heart would twist in two with love and desire.

This man had learned some dreadful lesson in the past. Maybe his childhood had been marred by warring parents. Maybe there was some relationship in his life she didn't know about that had further scarred him. But Beth was starting to see Kell Hallam through new eyes. She was starting to see that here was not only a man who was dangerous to her peace of mind, but a man who was alone and—and maybe as emotionally drained as she.

This was a new and strange lesson Beth was learning. She'd always held herself aloof from men—held herself as unworthy of a loving relationship. And yet...

Yet she could love this man. She could. She could love this man and this child—and maybe in doing so... If she agreed to marry him...

This was crazy thinking. Wishful fancy. Kell Hallam didn't need her—except as some sort of economical, sensible partner. Marriage by contract? What sort of marriage was that? There was only pain for Beth down that road.

Beth looked up at Kell and forced her mouth to twist into a smile. She lifted her glass in silent salute.

And in her heart a crazy germ of an idea was taking root. The sort of an idea that the Beth of yesterday would have dismissed as ludicrous. She wouldn't agree to a marriage of convenience. She wouldn't. But maybe... Dear heaven, maybe...

'If there's no danger in one glass—maybe I'd better have two,' she said lightly, and her eyes met his. There was just the slightest trace of defiance in her look. So far Kell had called all the shots here. So far...

Well, this was Beth's home. Beth's territory. And maybe she didn't have a lot to lose here. Nothing to lose—but everything to win.

The omelette seemed better than any Beth had tasted—maybe it was Kell's cooking that did it, or the wine that accompanied it, or the moment.

It was the wine, she told herself firmly. The wine was fabulous—rich and full of fruit and lingering on the tastebuds long after it had gone from her lips. Beth drank a glass—and then two—and then, as Kell poured a third and suggested they go out to the verandah to drink the last of the bottle, she didn't demur. The shy and frightened Beth Lister was being asked to take a step back—and wait and see.

The night had settled in properly while they'd eaten. The moon was a golden ball hanging low over the mountains. Its light was casting a swathe over the treetops, and was enough illumination on its own without the need for the porch light. Beth excused herself and let her wine glass be for a while as she saw to the needs of her animals, but when she returned Kell was just where she'd left him, sitting on the verandah rail looking out to the starlit sky.

'It's quite a place you have here,' he said softly as she

closed the screen door behind her and recovered her glass. 'You're really going to miss it.'

'There are other great places,' Beth said, a trifle unsteadily. 'Yours, for instance. Maybe one day I'll find another sanctuary.'

'You know my offer still stands,' Kell told her. 'You could move to my home—either as Katie's nanny or as my wife.'

'The terms being much the same for either position,' Beth said softly, and Kell nodded.

'The second position's more permanent,' he told her. 'But essentially, yes. You'd be free to run your life as you want it.'

It sounded as if he was offering her a great job. A job that made her feel so bleak...

'I don't want it,' she whispered. She took a sip of wine, and suddenly the wine didn't taste so good any more. She took a deep breath—and put her glass down. Crossing to the verandah rail, Beth swung herself up and over so that she was sitting beside Kell as he gazed out at the stars. It felt weirdly intimate—and yet horribly lonely.

Could she say it? Could she?

'I told you, Kell,' she said slowly. 'I can't accept marriage on those terms. Not when I'd have to live close to you. See you every day. Know that you'd be my husband—yet *not* my husband. It seems to me that what you're offering would be some sort of exquisite torture.'

'Torture...' Kell turned to face her in the moonlight. 'Beth, what the hell do you mean by that?'

It seemed she could say it. It seemed she had no choice.

'I mean I've started to fall in love with you,' Beth managed, and to her satisfaction her voice shook hardly at all. 'Heaven knows why, Kell Hallam. It's not something I intended to do. But when you kissed me last night something changed for me.

I've never felt this way…the way I feel now…about anyone in my life before, but I feel it about you.'

'Beth…'

'Look, I know you don't want this,' she said steadily, and made herself continue to stare out at the night sky instead of at the man beside her. 'I know you don't want what I'm offering. But I'm saying that you have it regardless. It's not something that you can give away at will. Love's something special. Something that just happens. I didn't understand that until now, but it's hit me like a sledgehammer and there's nothing I can do about it. So I just thought…you ought to know. That's all. That it's something you have—my love—regardless of whether you want it or not. That it's there.'

There was a long silence. Somewhere out in the night a mopoke was calling its weird, lonely song.

'I can't…' Kell said at last—and then stopped.

'You can't love me back?' Beth answered gently. 'I know that, Kell. But…even though we've known each other so little time I know what I feel—and I also know that you've asked me to marry you. I'm saying if you married me, Kell, then you'd have a wife who loved you. You'd have a proper wife. A woman who felt that she was a part of you. That's why…there's part of me that's saying I can't marry you—because of the way I feel—and there's another part of me that's saying I can't bear not to. That's just the way it is, Kell. Take it or leave it. But don't ask me to marry you again—without knowing… Don't…'

Beth faltered to a stop then, and closed her eyes. The night closed in around her, constricting her, and the mopoke's cry was like a dirge. It was the same feeling as being in a cage, with the wire confines gradually coming in—squeezing…

But it wasn't a cage doing the confining. It was Kell. Her love. While Beth closed her eyes the big man let himself slide forward from the verandah rail. Now he was standing before her on the grass, his strong hands lifting her down to stand before him. Beth opened her eyes in trepidation to look up at him—and found his troubled eyes looking straight back.

'Beth, this is crazy. You mustn't...'

'Love?' she whispered. She steadied on her feet in his grasp. 'I mustn't love? Is that what you're saying? It isn't possible, Kell. It isn't possible for me to stop loving.'

'I know it isn't,' he said gently. 'Not for someone like you. Love's your specialty, Beth, and I'd be a fool not to see it. But your love... Save it, Beth. Save it for your orphaned creatures—and for little ones like Katie. Save it for those who need it.'

'You don't need it?' There was a pain in Beth's heart that was almost unbearable. She was going to cry, she thought. This night... This man... The feel of his hands at her waist... Kell's very being....

Beth stood motionless in Kell's hold, and in his hold she felt right. She had known this man only two days—yet with him Beth felt a sense of belonging so great it was as if it would tear her in two to leave him. Or to have him leave her. But...

'I don't need it,' Kell said simply. 'I'm on my own, Beth.' He hesitated and gave an almost imperceptible shrug. 'Beth, despite my mistrust of marriage, I did try it once. It was a disaster. Joanne and I tore each other apart. She grew to hate the farm—to hate the isolation. Hate all the things I loved. And...'

'But, Kell, maybe she'd always hated them,' Beth argued desperately. Beth was fighting a battle with opponents she knew nothing of. Shadows of a past she could only guess at. 'Maybe you hadn't been honest with each other in the first place. Did you ever think of that?'

'Oh, yes, I thought of that,' Kell told her, his voice bleak. 'But...my mother...and then my wife... I'm not repeating the same mistakes, Beth. Not even for you. We marry on an emotionless contract or not at all.'

'That's not fair.'

'It's the way it has to be.' Kell's voice was as joyless as Beth's heart. 'I'll make no promises I can't keep, Bethany Lister, and if you can't keep your emotions in check—'

'Are you saying that *you* can keep your emotions under strict control?' A surge of anger came to Beth's aid then. She was right to be angry. This wasn't fair. He was here. Kell was still holding her—and he was still making her feel light-headed with desire. Kell made her feel like someone she hardly knew. Like someone capable of all the love in the world. Certainly she had enough love for two. It was only Kell's words that drove her off. Words...

So... If she couldn't fight with words...what else did she have to fight with?

Beth stared up at her love, reaching for a courage she hadn't known she possessed. Could she dare press on? Could she?

She could only try.

'Are you saying you can keep your emotions in check, Kell?' she said again, in a whisper. 'That you don't feel like I do—at least a little? That you don't feel anything in your heart when you hold me...or when you kiss me?' She shook her head. 'I'm sorry, Kell, but I don't believe you. I can't...'

And then, before she could stop herself—before her head found the sense to scream at her heart to stop—Beth stood on tiptoe and placed her lips firmly against his.

How could she do such a thing? Heaven knew. All Beth knew was that she'd done it—and the consequences were all around her.

Beth felt the shock at her touch run the entire length of Kell's long body. He responded involuntarily to Beth's kiss with a shudder that might almost have been one of revulsion.

Not quite. It wasn't revulsion. It wasn't. Kell's arms at

Beth's waist were still holding her, and as his body shuddered his mouth moved to accept her kiss.

And Beth's heart told her to keep on kissing. It was her only hope. It seemed like a rope thrown to a drowning man. Her desperate kiss was a link to what she wanted most in the world.

Please... Please...

And then, as if they had a life of their own, Kell's arms tightened in a convulsive grip.

And then it was Kell's call.

For that first brief moment it had been Beth who had kissed—Beth who had instigated passion—but suddenly no more. Somehow she'd struck some deep chord—caused some reaction that was stronger than the man she kissed—stronger than Beth—stronger than both of them combined.

And Beth was being pulled up so that Kell's mouth could claim her properly. His mouth was possessing her—taking the sweet offering of her lips and more—taking Beth's body to him with a need that was older than time itself.

Man and woman. One. A joining of two hearts into one. A merging of two bodies...

A flare of hope lit within Beth's heart and built as the feel of him intensified. Built to a flame. A white-hot heat. Beth's hands came up to cling to Kell's face—deepening the kiss, claiming him as hers. This was her right. Whatever Kell's voice might say, this man in her arms was *her* man. This man wanted her. He needed her—and every fibre of his body was screaming the truth of what her heart was telling her.

And Beth's body was replying. She could feel joy blasting through her as Kell's kiss claimed her entirely—as his hands pulled her closer—closer—so that the softness of her breasts was moulded into the hard-muscled strength of his chest.

And then Kell's hands were moving, feeling under the soft fabric of Beth's T-shirt—finding the smooth curves of her breasts and the tautness of each nipple. Beth's body was responding with every fibre of its being to the man holding her—and her proudly erect breasts were declaration enough of her need. She let her own hands fall again, to slip underneath Kell's shirt. The feel of his naked skin made her tremble. The smell of him…the sense of him…

How could he drive her away—this man who was her other half? How could he?

Beth's hand slipped inexorably down to the button of Kell's jeans. She fingered it for three whole seconds before it came undone—and then her fingers were sliding down—down—until they came to what she had been searching for.

And Kell's body stilled into frozen shock.

She wouldn't let him draw back. She wouldn't. Beth's fingers teased—pleased—desired. And with joy she felt his absolute response. His body couldn't lie—even though his voice could declare him unmoved. She knew better.

'Kell,' Beth whispered desperately. 'Kell…love me. Please, Kell…'

She pulled his head down to hers—down—down—pressuring his body to come down to her. 'Kell, I want you.' Beth's voice was a husky whisper under his lips. 'I want you more than anything I've ever wanted in my entire life. For now…'

'Beth, you don't know what you're doing…' Somehow he pulled away enough to answer her. It was a protest, but there was an answering passion in Kell's words. His voice cracked in his response—a man torn almost in two by need.

'Yes, I do.' Beth's voice was suddenly sure. 'Yes, I do know what I'm doing, Kell. I know you don't want me as a proper wife. I know you don't want me for ever. I know tomorrow you'll leave here, and I'm not asking you to stay. But for tonight…for tonight let me love you, Kell. Let me love you as I want to. And love me back. Just for tonight.'

'Beth…'

'Kell, you don't have to worry about pregnancy,' Beth said softly, raising one hand to lovingly finger the roughness of his coarse, sun-bleached hair. 'I'm protected. I made sure... I didn't trust Lyle—once we were married—so I...'

Mistake.

As soon as she'd said Lyle's name, Beth knew that to do so had been a mistake. She felt Kell's body stiffen. Her mention of Lyle's name shook Kell back into reality faster than anything else could have done. Beth felt her words slam into his consciousness and his body become rigid—and before she could protest both her hands were held in a grip of iron and she was pushed away from his body.

'Beth, what the hell are you saying?' Kell stepped back and stared—his eyes black and fathomless in the moonlight.

'I'm...' Beth faltered. As Kell released his hold she stumbled and had to fight to stop herself from falling. Her hands came out in an involuntary protest at Kell's rejection—and then came back to hang uselessly at her sides. Beth's courage—so high a moment ago—took a step closer to failing absolutely as she moved.

'I...I didn't want to sleep with Lyle,' she whispered in desolation. 'But he'd made passes at me before. More than passes, really. I thought...if we were legally married I might have trouble stopping him. I might not... And it would have been a disaster if he'd raped me and I'd got pregnant. So I...'

'So you prepared yourself for your husband,' Kell said flatly. 'Fiancé number one. And now you're offering yourself to another potential husband. What's the price this time, Beth?'

Kell's words slashed cruelly down—and Beth put a hand to her face as if to ward off the hurt.

'No.'

Beth shook her head, her hair falling in soft tendrils over her face in her distress. She swept the curls back, only to have them fall straight down again, and a wave of desolation swept over her that was so great she felt ill.

This wasn't going to work. She had taken an impossible risk. She had offered more than she had ever offered in her life before—and she had failed.

Kell didn't trust her. By the sound of his voice now he didn't even like her.

How could she have hoped so desperately that he could learn to love her?

'I'm—I'm sorry, Kell,' she faltered. 'I shouldn't have…'

'No, you shouldn't.' Bleak. Cold. Cruel.

'Then forget… Forget I said…'

She couldn't make her voice work one moment longer. It was all just too much. Beth gave a tiny, choking sob and turned away.

'I think you should go to bed, Beth.' The cruel tone had gone from Kell's voice—but the words were still flat, harsh, devoid of all expression. 'I think it would be best for both of us if we went our separate ways. I'm sorry if by proposing marriage I made you hope there could ever be anything else. There isn't. We'll leave first thing in the morning. Goodnight, Beth.'

Beth closed her eyes. She willed the ground to open at her feet—open and swallow her and close mercifully over her.

It didn't. She had to make her feet move up the verandah steps—up and away and into the house.

Away from the man whom she loved more than life itself—and who didn't want anything to do with her.

Beth's verandah was no place for sleeping.

Kell abandoned his air mattress. He'd only brought it for Katie, and there was no way its comfort could help him sleep tonight. After Beth disappeared into the house he spent a long time staring sightlessly out into the darkness—then took his bedroll from the back of his car and walked out into the night.

Out under the gums he might find the solitude he craved. The peace…

If there was any place in the world to find peace it was here. Five hundred yards from the house the cleared paddocks turned to wilderness. Generations of littered gum leaves from the towering trees provided a soft enough mattress, and the warm night air was full of the scent of the bush. There was the odd call of the lonely mopoke—but that was all the noise there was. Only the stars and moon kept him company.

An hour later Kell was still awake. Two hours later nothing had changed. Then three… Normally Kell slept like the dead out in the bush. The bush was his love.

His love.

It was his only love, Kell told himself bleakly over and over as he lay with his hands linked under his head and watched the stars through the canopy of leaves above his head. He'd been raised to be a bushman. He always had the bush as his constant companion. The bush was always there—dependable—lovely—a friend even in the bleakest of times.

This country's all I want, he told himself flatly, thrusting away the vision of Beth Lister's warmth and gentle loveliness. It's all…

But he had Katie now, though—regardless, Kell was forced to remind himself. His barriers had been breached. He was no longer impregnable. The love that was starting to grow inside him for his little ward was something he had fought against for so long—something he had vowed never to try to find again—but, no matter what he had promised himself, his love for Katie was something he could do nothing about. Katie was demanding to be loved and there was no choice for Kell to make. He must give his love in return.

But he didn't have to extend that love to Beth as well. To

let himself love a woman… That was to expose himself to all
the hurt he had sworn he would never face again. And to
expose Katie to the risks of being a child in such a marriage?
He deliberately let another small face drift across his thoughts
and the pain of remembering hardened his heart. He knew he
couldn't expose Katie in such a way. Never.

But Beth's face was still there above him in the starlight.
Wistful, loving, helpless…

He could love her. Dear God, he could love her. Kell's body
shifted restlessly on his bedroll and he found his gaze turning
towards the house. Beth was there. Five hundred yards away.
Beth was soft and compliant and loving—and she had given
herself to him without reservation. He knew without being told
how much she had given of herself in her one effort to seduce
him. He had thrust her away as he might have thrust a whore—
but he knew in his heart that Beth was no such thing. She
seemed… An innocent?

Well, innocent or not, he had thrust her away with as much
cruelty as he could muster. Thrust her away because to have
done anything else would only mean more hurt in the long
run. More pain.

Kell had carefully built himself a life that was full and satisfying. He had his land and his animals and the work he
loved.

And now he had Katie to love—and to protect.

Dear God, that was enough for any man who had been
through what he had endured. It had to be enough. Beth didn't
know what she was asking. She couldn't. The barriers Kell
had built had been constructed by years of pain and desolation.
He couldn't let them crumble now. Not for one chit of a girl
who spoke with her heart instead of her head.

Crazy, crazy, crazy.

If only he could sleep! Kell's heart twisted within at the
desolation that had been with him for years. He stared out for

one more long moment at the distant cottage. There was an urge inside him to leave his bedroll, walk over to the cottage, go straight into Beth's bedroom and sweep her compliant love-liness up into his arms. To make he and Beth and Katie—and even the odd wallaby and possum and echidna—one united family.

To accept Beth's love with a joyous heart.

The urge was so strong it was almost a compulsion.

But the mopoke sounded again—and its plaintive cry brought Kell back to reality.

There was no joy down that road. Dear God, hadn't he learned his lesson by now?

I've been a fool once in my life, he told himself savagely, twisting his body to face the darkness away from the cottage. Once. No more. Keep your head, Kell Hallam—and get the hell away from here as fast as you possibly can.

Get away from here before your heart takes over—and makes decisions you'll regret for the rest of your life.

CHAPTER TEN

KELL and Katie left Beth's cottage before eight the following morning.

'I've told the men I'll be back by lunchtime,' Kell told his niece when she protested violently. 'We have to get the hay out and—'

'Mr Craig can get the hay out,' Katie protested. She sat up in Beth's kitchen in front of a soft-boiled egg and stirred it without interest. 'He always does. Why do you have to do it today?'

'Mr Craig's still on holidays,' Kell said flatly. 'Finish your egg, Katie. We have to go—now.'

Kell hardly looked at Beth—and she hardly looked at him. What was between them from the night before was too raw for either to face head-on. After making sure their breakfast was okay Beth left them to work with her animals until Kell and Karie were ready to leave. Then, reluctantly, she came out to the car to say goodbye.

And Katie flung her arms round Beth's neck and burst into tears.

'I'll never see you again,' she sobbed. 'I never will.'

'Of course you will.' Beth bit her lip, nearly as torn by the pain in the little girl's voice as she was by the pain round her own heart. Somehow Beth forced herself to look up to Kell. 'What if I came to your home in a few weeks and took Katie for an overnight holiday—all on her own?' She wiped the tears from the little girl's eyes. 'Would your Uncle Kell allow that?' she asked the child.

Katie turned a tear-stained face to Kell. 'Can I, Uncle Kell?'

146

Then she frowned. 'But...does it have to be by myself? Wouldn't you want to come too, Uncle Kell?'

'I'm usually busy on the farm, Katie,' Kell told her, gently removing the child from Beth's clasp and lifting her into his arms. In this way Katie seemed a shield between man and woman. Someone to focus on so they didn't have to focus on each other. 'But I don't see why you shouldn't come and visit Beth,' he assured the child. 'It's very kind of Beth to offer.'

Kind.

It might be kind, Beth thought bleakly, but Kell's words were impersonal. Cold and ungiving.

Beth bit her lip, fighting to keep tears from her eyes.

'I might not be able to bring you here, Katie,' Beth warned, the desolation in her heart threatening to overpower her. 'I don't own this farm. But wherever I am I'll come in a month or so to visit you, Katie-bell,' she promised.

Kell's brow snapped down in a frown. 'You are definitely leaving the farm, then?'

'I have no choice.' As Kell opened his mouth to say something more Beth silenced him with a shake of her head. 'No real choice.' She gave a tight smile. 'I promised you I won't marry Lyle—and I won't go back on my word now. Even for my animals.'

'But...Beth, you won't have trouble with Lyle?' Kell's voice cut across Beth's self-pity and she had to blink as she tried to focus on what he meant.

Lyle... Lyle was a world away.

'No-No. I'll be fine.' She swallowed. 'You'd better go, then. The hay... The cattle...'

'Yes... The cattle need to be fed.' Kell shook his head, as if to shake off a bad dream. 'We have to go. Thank you for your hospitality, Beth.'

It was the last thing he said to her. Katie was strapped into the back seat—and there was a long moment of silence as Kell and Beth looked at each other from opposite sides of the car.

Nothing.

Then he was gone. Beth was left alone to her future.

And Kell drove away feeling he had just been offered something so precious most men would take it with open arms—but him...

He had responded by driving his boot in hard. He had responded with cruel rejection. It was the way it had to be.

The victim of a driving boot was just what Beth felt like. She felt as if she had been savagely beaten—bruised in mind and spirit. What now?

What indeed?

The next few days passed in a blur of misery as Beth took stock of her life and tried to adjust to the changes she must make.

She couldn't stay here. There simply wasn't any money coming in to pay the rent. And if she had to move...

Her last big kangaroo had just been released into the wild and her little wallabies were soon due to start their acclimatisation process into the bush. If Beth started their programme here then she'd be forced to stay on for a couple more months until they no longer needed her. And she couldn't afford to pay the lease for that long.

So, after days of soul-searching, she finally packed up her dependent little charges and took them down the coast—a journey of fifty miles—to where an elderly couple ran another animal shelter similar to hers. These people had helped in her training. They were friends—and they were both pleased to see her and upset to know the fate of her shelter.

'Oh, Beth, you've tried so hard,' Edna Walter said sadly as she helped Beth unload her little creatures from the car. 'It's not fair.'

'I know it's not,' Beth agreed. She lifted her two little wallabies from their padded travelling cages and gave them a swift hug as she moved them into their new home. 'But it can't be helped. I'm just glad you've been able to take them all.'

Edna surveyed her young friend with a worried air. 'Well, you've found a home for your charges—but what about you, Beth? Where will you go?' She surveyed her living room, which looked very similar to Beth's cluttered parlour. 'You could stay here with us for a while,' she suggested gently. 'With such a big influx of creatures we could do with some help.'

'You don't really mean that.' Beth smiled at her elderly friend's concerned face, recognising the kindness that had driven Edna to make the offer. 'You know you and Fred thrive on being busy. You coped after the bushfires last year and you coped magnificently. You know you don't need me.'

'But where will you go?'

Beth shook her head. 'Back to earning my living,' she said sadly. 'You know as well as anyone that you need capital to do this job—and there's no way to earn capital except by working. I'll try the vet practice where I used to work...'

'Move back to the city?' Edna's brow furrowed. 'But you're a bush girl, Beth. You can't survive in the city.'

'I survived in the city for years,' Beth told her. 'I can do it again.'

'But...' Edna's wise old eyes surveyed her friend with care. 'I don't know. There's something...Beth, you seem so alone.' She sighed. 'Maybe what's happened has been for the best. Maybe it's time you got off the farm. Met a few young people. Had a boyfriend...'

'I don't want...'

But Edna's eyes were crinkling at the sight of the changes in Beth's face. 'There.' She sighed with delight at her perception. 'I knew it. You *are* different. You've met someone, haven't you, Beth?'

'How did…?'

'I've known you a long time.' Edna concentrated on Beth's face. 'So…who is he and why are you looking sad?'

'Because there's nothing in it,' Beth whispered. 'You're right, Edna. I have met someone. But he doesn't want me. He doesn't want anyone.'

'Then the man's a fool,' Edna said roundly. 'I'll tell him so if you like. Who is he?'

'No one you've met,' Beth managed. 'No one who moves in our circles. He has nothing to do with me, Edna. Wanting him—loving him—is like whistling for the moon. Just as hopeless. I've just got to get myself over it as best I can…and start again.'

Without her animals, Beth's farm seemed an empty shell. There were only the hens and Daisy and her kid left. Beth took Daisy over to the neighbouring farm. The people there also ran cashmere goats and were delighted at the addition to their herd—even a goat as ill-tempered as Daisy. They took Beth's hens as well. Then there was nothing to do but pack up her belongings and try to find a job and somewhere to live in the city.

First, though, she had to give her landlord notice, and that seemed so final. Beth spent a night staring at a huge open-air fire made from wood from the tree she and Kell had cut. At least *that* was a source of satisfaction—the tree could provide heat and comfort for years rather than lying at the bottom of the dam, and even though the person heated and comforted by it wouldn't be Beth, she still found the thought good. She spent the whole night out under the stars by her fire, and the next morning she drove into town to give notice to quit the place.

When she did, the estate agent stared at her as if she was crazy.

The man listened to her story for thirty seconds, his face growing more and more puzzled, and then he cut across Beth's words.

'Miss Lister, I don't understand. How can you hand in your notice when you now own the farm?'

'Own…?'

'I had a telephone call from the owners three days ago,' he told her, still frowning. 'They said they'd been given an offer they couldn't refuse for the place—and the new owner was the previous tenant, Miss Bethany Lister. They advised me to destroy the lease and to take the property off our books.'

'But…'

'I'm sure I haven't made a mistake,' the agent said. 'They confirmed it by fax the same morning, so I have it in writing if you'd like to see. Oh, and there's also another letter here for you, marked ''personal''. It arrived here yesterday, with a covering note saying that as the sender didn't have your postal address could we forward it to you.'

The agent sifted through a pile of papers on his desk until he found what he was looking for, adjusted the spectacles on his long nose, handed the letter over and waited.

Beth stared at the man before her with unseeing eyes. He gazed back with detached interest, waiting for her reaction.

Waiting for her to open her letter.

Beth looked down at the heavy bond paper. Her fingers trembled, she noted. All she had to do was rip and read… All…

And finally she did.

With our thanks. We owe you this, Beth. Our only stipulation is a requirement for an occasional holiday for Katie-bell.

Katie and Kell.

And attached to the note was the title for her farm.

For a long, long moment Beth didn't even breathe. She couldn't. She stood staring stupidly down at the paper before her, as though somehow by staring at it she could make it into sense.

Kell had bought her farm. He was giving it to her. A gift worth thousands...

We owe you this, the note said.

He owed her nothing.

'Would you like a chair?' All of a sudden the agent seemed concerned. Beth looked up at him with eyes that were dazed with shock. She must look pale, she thought. She could feel the blood drain away from her face.

'N-no. I'm sorry.' She shook her head, fighting to find some semblance of common sense. 'Look...this is a mistake. I guess there has been a change of ownership, but the new owner is a man called Kell Hallam.'

The estate agent took the title deeds from Beth's nerveless grasp.

'It says *your* name on these papers, miss,' he corrected her. 'It doesn't say anything about anyone called Kell Hallam.'

'Nevertheless...' Beth took a deep breath. 'Nevertheless, that's who the land belongs to. If you'll excuse me, I need to sort it out. Mr Hallam's made a mistake.'

'You do that, miss,' the agent said gently, a look of concern on his normally acquisitive face. 'But there's no need to worry about the rent while you're doing your sorting. As far as I'm concerned the land belongs to you. If you have some rich sugar-daddy out there, doling out presents, if I were you I'd just say, Thanks very much, and get on with it. That's what I'd do.'

Maybe.

But it wasn't what she could do, Beth thought miserably, turning her little car northwards as she left town. If Kell Hallam wanted to play sugar-daddy then he could do it to someone else. She wasn't living on land boughtby him because he felt he owed her. That was making money from Lyle's greediness just as surely as marrying Lyle would have been. Until a week ago Beth had never met Kell Hallam. Now... Now she was so tied up with him in her heart that she thought she'd go mad.

And she didn't want to add boundless gratitude toher emotions.

Beth decided to make the journey to Kell's farm on the spur of the moment. Unfortunately she forgot one essential fact.

She forgot exactly where Kell's farm was.

She'd travelled there once. It was somewhere in the Blue Mountains north of Sydney, she knew. Well and good. She remembered she'd passed through the little town of Cooneera a few miles south of the farm. That was fine. She could find Cooneera—but after Cooneera she found herself hopelessly lost.

All the roads in the bush looked the same, she thought desperately, turning up one bush track after another. The journey to and from Kell's farm had been undertaken when Beth was emotionally fraught. The last things she'd been paying attention to were signposts and landscapes.

Now she cursed herself for a fool and finally turned back towards Cooneera. It had taken her all afternoon to travel here in her ancient car. Now it was growing dark. Facing Kell would have to wait until morning. If she wasn't to spend the night in the car she had to find somewhere to stay.

Cooneera was hardly worthy of the description 'town'. The

place boasted a general store, a tiny schoolhouse nestled deep in the bush, two well tended churches and one decrepit pub.

Country pubs were obliged to have rooms to let. Beth eyed the dilapidated building with caution, but she had no choice. It was stay in the Cooneera pub for the night or give up and go home.

'Give up and go home' sounded good to her at the moment. But that was the coward's way out. Beth couldn't just meekly accept Kell's gift of a farm. She couldn't live with such undeserved and overwhelming generosity. So, sighing with tiredness, she parked her car alongside a row of tray trucks and four-wheel drives in front of the pub and made her way inside.

To her surprise, the inside of the pub was much classier than its exterior. The saloon was clean and inviting, with the group of drinkers clustered along the bar being the one untidy element to the place.

The customers were all men. As Beth entered they turned as one to check the newcomer out. Beth had to fight rising colour as the men realized they'd been joined by an attractive young woman and their inspection turned to blatant appreciation.

Australian country pubs were still very much a male domain, Beth thought ruefully, trying hard to stay composed as she walked across to the bar. Somewhere out at the back of the building there'd be a ladies' lounge, she knew, most likely with a floral beer-stained carpet, cobwebs, and the mustiness of disuse. On a Saturday night the ladies' lounge might see an occasional visitor—and the visitor's description would hardly be 'lady'—but if Beth walked into the ladies' lounge now she could be there all night before she attracted any attention.

Now, though… Now Beth had the attention of every drinker in the place—and the attention of the hotel-keeper as well. The middle-aged woman behind the bar was also looking at

Beth, and, as a young buck ventured a wolf whistle and a leering look at Beth, the woman aimed a dishcloth at her cheeky customer's head. The dishcloth was sodden and deadly accurate.

'That'll be enough out of you, Ted Barnett,' the woman said severely as Ted's mates fell about laughing. 'You leave the girl alone.' Then she turned her back on his soggy protests. 'Yes, miss?' she enquired of Beth. 'How can I help you?'

'I'd like a room for the night,' Beth managed—and the room erupted again. Offers of hospitality came from all sides—and none of the offers coming from the drinkers were the least bit respectable. The lady hotel-keeper, however, was more than equal to any of her noisy customers in making herself heard.

'One more word from you lot and the pub's dry 'til next Monday,' she interjected loudly. She put her hands on her hips and glared. 'And don't think I don't mean it, boys. I'm within my rights to serve what I please. Any more cheek to the young lady and it's lemonade all round.'

There was a deathly hush. The men looked from Beth to their hostess, took the measure of the middle-aged hotel keeper—and then their conversations hurriedly resumed where they'd left off when Beth entered. Beth was suddenly non-existent. Lemonade was a dire threat indeed.

Then, as the focus moved away from Beth, the hotel-keeper came out from behind the bar and ushered Beth from the room.

'Take no notice of them, dear,' the woman told Beth kindly. 'They've just been given their shearing cheques and they've all had a few. Believe it or not, they've nearly all got wives and kiddies at home—and if you looked like taking their offers seriously they'd run a mile. Now... Let me show you our rooms. They're clean and comfortable—and I sleep at the head of the stairs so they're also safe as houses.'

Without waiting for Beth to respond, she led the way to a

bright little bedroom on the first floor, then turned to Beth with enquiring eyes. 'The cost of the room is thirty dollars including breakfast. Dinner's five dollars extra and it's pie and chips or steak and chips.' Then she relented a little. 'But I can do a salad if you like, dear. It'll make a nice change.'

'Thank you,' Beth told her. 'But I wonder also… The reason I'm here is that I'm lost,' she confessed. 'I've spent the afternoon trying to find a farm. I've given up for the day—it's too late to arrive now—but I'd like to find it in the morning.'

'Whose farm?' the landlady asked. 'I reckon within a thirty-mile radius I know everyone—right down to the ancestry of their mongrel dogs. There's not a lot I don't hear of in this bar.'

'I suppose there's not.' Beth smiled wearily. 'The place I'm looking for belongs to Kell Hallam.'

'Kell Hallam…' The landlady's bright interest sharpened even more. She paused, and for the first time she seemed to take full stock of Beth. Beth was wearing clean jeans and a neat pastel shirt, her curls were tied decorously back and she looked respectable enough—but it wasn't Beth's respectability that seemed in question here. 'Kell Hallam,' the landlady breathed in satisfaction. 'Then I'll just bet you're the new lady everyone's been talking about.'

'New lady…' Beth frowned. 'I'm sorry. I don't know what you mean.'

'You must be our Kell's new lady.' The landlady smiled at Beth's obvious discomfiture. 'You can't hide anything round here, dear—and the whole district knows there's a woman on the scene. We're so glad for him! It's time that nice man had a decent break for a change.'

'I don't…'

'Now don't say I'm not right.' The woman's eyes were watching Beth's mounting colour with satisfaction. 'I can see

I've hit a nerve. You don't colour up like that when there's nothing going on.'

'But...but how...'

'Ten days ago Kell Hallam told all his employees that he wanted the place to himself for a few days,' the woman told her. 'He gave them all paid leave. Then someone saw him driving through the town with a woman in the car—a lady with curly red-brown hair. Next thing we know she's left and he's off after her—had to call his people back so he could go. And since then...

'Well, his little niece that everyone thought was mute has been talking like a butcher's magpie. They tell me you can't stop her. And it's all about Beth this and Beth that. And the guys who work on the place say Kell's going round looking like he's been slapped in the face by a wet fish. Now...' The hotel-keeper folded her arms over her ample bosom and fixed Beth with a look. 'Is or is not your name Beth?'

'I...' Beth swallowed. 'Yes,' she whispered.

'Well...' The woman sighed, and there was all the love of romance a woman could muster in the sigh. 'Beth... What a pretty name. And now you've come back.' She sighed again. 'Well, I'll be wishing you all the best, my dear, and I'll do my bit to smooth your path. There's no charge tonight. Not one red cent. If you can cheer our Kell Hallam up...take that dear little mite of a Katie under your wing and make them both happy...'

'Mrs...'

'Trotter.' The woman beamed. 'Madge Trotter.'

'Mrs Trotter, I don't know what you're talking about,' Beth said helplessly. 'You're going way too fast. I hardly know Kell Hallam.'

'You've stayed at his farm, though?'

'Y-yes.'

'And he's stayed at yours?'

'Yes, but…'

'Well, my pa would have married me off at the end of a shotgun on less grounds than that,' Mrs Trotter said roundly. 'Don't you mess our Kell around, girl. After all that man's been through…'

Beth took a deep breath. She felt as if she was back in Kell's mud, sinking deeper every minute. 'Mrs Trotter, I don't…I don't…' She ran out of steam and looked helplessly at Madge Trotter's stern face. 'I don't know…'

'What don't you know?'

Beth closed her eyes. 'Tell me,' she said softly, but a part of her felt as if she had absolutely no right to ask the question. She couldn't fail to ask, though. 'Tell me what you mean when you say Kell's been through a lot,' she said slowly. 'You mean because his sister died and he and his first wife divorced?'

Silence.

Beth cautiously opened her eyes again to find Madge Trotter looking at her in stupefaction.

'You mean you don't know?'

'Don't know what?' Beth said helplessly. 'Mrs Trotter, it's true I don't know Kell Hallam very well. We only met ten days ago and I…'

'You're dotty about him, though—aren't you?'

The woman's eyes were on Beth's face, and Beth couldn't lie. 'Yes,' she said simply. 'And I know there are shadows. But I don't know what they are.'

'You could have asked anyone hereabouts. Any local would have told you.'

'I don't know anyone local. Except you. Will you tell me?'

Madge Trotter sucked in air between her teeth. She looked at Beth for a long moment, as though taking her measure, and then she walked out to the head of the stairs. 'Roy!' she yelled, in a voice that would have woken the dead within a radius of ten miles. 'Mind the bar!' Then she walked back into Beth's bedroom and closed the door.

'I'll tell you what you're fighting,' she said bluntly. 'It's that damned first wife of his. Joanne. Married too young, they did—and Joanne was out for nothing but his looks and his money. Well, she got tired of that pretty soon, I can tell you, and the stories that started about her... Well, I won't bore you with them.'

'But she left,' Beth said cautiously. 'I can't see... Are you saying that Kell still loves her?'

'I shouldn't imagine he loved her twelve months after he married her,' Madge said stoutly. 'The way she acted it'd have taken a fool to keep loving her. But he did the right thing by her. Kept taking her back time after time when she left. But the last time... The last time she left she took what he loved more than life itself, they say. What broke his heart...'

'What...?'

'She took their daughter,' Madge said softly. 'That was why Kell kept taking Joanne back—because of the little one. He loved the child so much, and Joanne was her mother. But the last time... The last time Joanne lost her temper and stormed off with the little one before Kell could stop her. She'd never taken the child before—never wanted her—but this time they say she did it just to punish Kell. Only she didn't take her far. She ran off the road just twenty miles from the farm. Driving a stupid, fast little sports car and going twice the speed limit. And she killed them both.'

It was a long time before Beth slept that night, and she woke feeling as if she hadn't slept at all. She lay in the dawn stillness and the troubles of the night crowded back on her as an overwhelming sadness.

How to fight shadows like these? Beth had thought she was unhappy losing the farm. How much more had Kell lost?

Kell...

How much had he suffered? How much had it cost him to go to a foreign country and bring home a little girl who was not his daughter? To open himself to a child again and let himself love her? To take her to his heart?

And here was Beth—asking him to take her as well. Love her... Expose himself all over again to the pain he'd felt at his betrayal and loss.

Maybe he thought he couldn't let his heart go. To expose himself again was also to put Katie at risk. He'd made a dreadful mistake in the past. Who could blame him for acting only with his head now?

He'd offered to marry her, Beth thought bleakly, and wondered what sort of marriage contract Kell had had in mind when he'd made the offer. She could just bet there'd be a strong proviso written in that gave her no power whatsoever over Katie's future.

Dear heaven... What was she to do now?

Get out of bed and go to see him, she told herself bleakly. Give him back the title of his gifted land—and make one last attempt... One last attempt to be a part of his life. To make him see that he could trust her. And if he couldn't? Then she had to find the strength to walk away—because to hurt Kell would cost her more than her life was worth.

CHAPTER ELEVEN

KELL was home.

Kell Hallam was out in the yard as Beth pulled to a halt in front of his house—and it was all she could do not to turn tail and flee.

She'd geared herself up to stop the car, take three deep breaths and then walk over to the house. Knock on the door and wait. Maybe even find Kell not home.

Instead he was standing by the stables overseeing the unloading of a small black mare from a horsebox. He looked up as Beth's car arrived—and didn't move. His face didn't break into a smile of welcome. It simply stilled.

So did Beth's heart. Dear God, how to handle this...? Please?

'H-hi,' she managed, and somehow persuaded her numb body to respond enough to get herself out of the car. 'I thought... Kell, I hope you don't mind me coming, but...I need to see you.'

'What about?'

As a welcome this was about as warming as a bucket of iced water. Beth flinched. She reached down and retrieved a wad of papers from the passenger seat of her car and held them out towards him.

'This,' she managed, and her voice sounded tight and strained. 'Your gift. I'm here to say that I can't take it. I don't want it. I never did, Kell, and you have to take it back.'

There was another man inside the horsebox. He came out now as Kell held out the reins of the mare he was holding.

'Take her and settle her in the stables, Charlie,' Kell said curtly. 'I'll be a minute. Come into the office, Miss Lister. I'd prefer that you didn't meet my niece while you're here.'

Beth cringed. Dear heaven...

There was no longer even a hint of friendship here. What had he called her? Miss Lister? The name was so cold. Formal. She was now reduced to a business acquaintance—no more. Without a further word Kell led her to a building at the end of the house and ushered her inside. And all the time Beth's heart grew colder.

'Now, Miss Lister...' Kell sat himself down on a chair on the far side of a vast desk and motioned to her to take the chair opposite. A sea of polished wood separated them. 'You told Katie you'd see her in about a month and I hadn't expected to hear from you until then. What seems to be the problem?'

'Kell, don't—'

'Tell me what you want, Beth,' Kell snapped. 'I'm busy.'

Beth bit her lip. She couldn't fight this. She couldn't.

'I just wanted to say that I don't want your gift,' she told him. She placed the title deeds of her farm on the desk before them. 'Kell...I've found homes for my animals. I've given my notice that I'm leaving. By the end of the week I'll have no further use for my farm and it doesn't belong to me. You...please, you mustn't give it to me. I have no right...'

'I owe it to you, Beth,' Kell said roughly. 'Your action in not marrying Mayberry has meant my niece inherits what's rightfully hers—and you persuaded her to talk again. I'm grateful and I pay my debts. Accept it.'

'You're buying me off,' Beth told him. 'I won't take this to salve your conscience, Kell Hallam.'

'What do you mean...buying you off? I had no—'

'You're paying me off because you won't love me,' Beth managed, fighting for every word. Her throat felt blocked from within. 'You're afraid of loving me. You're scared I'll turn into another Joanne. Hurt you. Maybe even hurt Katie like Joanne hurt your own little girl. You won't trust—'

'Who the hell told you about Joanne?'

'It doesn't matter who told me,' Beth said bleakly. 'But I know. I know what Joanne did to you, and Kell...I'm so sorry.'

'You don't have to be sorry.' Kell's face was flint-hard. 'Joanne's death and...and Laura's were a long time ago.'

'You still hurt because of it,' Beth whispered. 'To lose your little girl... To have Joanne betray you both like that... Kell, it must hurt so much—to start again. To pick up the pieces and go on. But, Kell, that's what you must do. You already love Katie—'

'And that's all I'm going to do,' Kell said savagely. 'Beth, don't you see that you're asking the impossible? To ask that I trust you...'

'Kell, if you love me then you will trust me, regardless of what your head tells you to do,' Beth answered him. 'And, Kell, what you're asking me to accept is even harder than me asking for your trust. You ask me to accept the fact that I love you and also accept your belief that I could hurt you and hurt Katie as Joanne did you and Laura. You must know...Kell, you *must* know I could never hurt you. Oh, Kell, I'd die rather. I'd die...'

She could say no more. There were tears welling behind Beth's eyes, but some semblance of pride held them back. She sat, white-faced and silent, and watched the stern, forbidding features of the man before her.

Kell didn't give an inch. Not one. His face didn't relent in its harshness. He sat there—judge and jury rolled into one— and Beth was condemned without her uttering a word.

She had to go. She had to go before she finally did burst into tears and made even more of a fool of herself. Somehow she managed to shove the title deeds across the desk and get herself to her feet.

'Take your land back,' she whispered. 'That's all I ask, and that's why I came. I don't want your conscience money. I told you before, Kell. I don't love for gain. And if I took this land I'd feel sick every day I lived on it.'

'What will you do?' Kell's hand came out to take the deeds. His voice was impersonal—as if she hadn't touched him one bit. Beth walked to the door and looked back. Somehow she managed to tilt her chin and find a trace of defiance.

'What I do is nothing to do with you, Kell Hallam. Not now. I just want to get as far away from you as possible and…and start again.'

'The title will be here if you change your mind.'

'I won't change my mind,' Beth said quietly. 'On some things I can be just as implacable as you.' She shrugged. 'And maybe just as bloody stupid!'

Beth left Kell believing his reaction had been cold and emotionless. Her impression was just about as far from the truth as it was possible to get.

For a long time after Beth left, Kell didn't move. He sat with his head in his hands, staring at the closed door, his mind numb.

Was what he was doing crazy? To send Beth away?

Kell had shoved a shield up in front of himself and he wasn't lowering it one bit, even though his heart was screaming at him that he was making a huge mistake.

'I can't risk Katie,' he told the stillness around him, and the words didn't even make sense to the silence.

All he had to do was lower the shield… Follow Beth… Gather her to him and love her…

And expose himself all over again. Lay open his heart and wait for the pain to begin.

It had already begun. The pain was all around him now.

'You're being stupid—cruel—criminal,' he said bleakly to the silence, and no one answered him. No one denied his accusation.

If I love her and she goes... Kell was talking to himself—talking to the young Kell Hallam, who had made a disastrous mistake the first time he'd chosen a wife and who'd paid for it with the life of his daughter. The memory of his loss rose up and almost overwhelmed him. It was the agony of memory that kept him glued to the spot. That stopped him launching himself out the door after Beth.

Beth wouldn't hurt you. She wouldn't hurt Katie. Dear heaven, Hallam, trust yourself. Trust your judgement. She's a girl in a million. A billion...

You trusted your judgement when you married Joanne. And look where it landed you.

This is different. Beth is so different...

But if you make another mistake... To expose yourself to hurt again... To expose Katie... To love and lose again is the way of madness.

'Why didn't Beth come to see me?'

The words were a plaintive whisper from the doorway, cutting across Kell's monologue with himself, and they made him jolt back to reality with a sickening start. He hauled his mind away from the vision of Beth's stricken face and saw Katie in the doorway, her eyes huge with confusion.

'Katie-bell...'

'I saw Beth,' Katie told him. 'I saw her from my bedroom window but she was getting into her car, and by the time I reached the yard she was gone. And she didn't come to see me.'

'It's not a month yet,' Kell said blankly. 'She said she'd come in a month.'

'But she was here now. She came now. Why didn't she stay?'

'Katie, Beth doesn't belong here,' Kell said dully. He rose and crossed to lift the little girl into his arms. 'Katie-bell, it's just you and me who live here. We're…we're family. Beth is a really nice lady, but she's just a visitor. Not…not one of us.'

Odd how such a reasoned statement could sound so desolate.

And Katie was shaking her head.

'Beth *is* one of us,' she said firmly. 'And, Uncle Kell, Beth was crying. I could see her crying from my window. She was crying and I wanted to give her a cuddle. But she went before I could reach her. Uncle Kell, Beth needs us just like we need her.'

'We don't need—'

'Yes, we *do*, Uncle Kell.' Katie's voice was suddenly strong. She wriggled away from him, demanding to be put down, and Kell obliged. Then his small niece stood before him, the expression on her face changing from confusion to anger.

'We *do* need Beth,' she said strongly—accusingly. 'Beth is our Beth. She gives us cuddles and she loves us and she makes us happy. When she was here it was almost the same as having Mummy again. And you laughed and so did she, and even the dogs thought Beth was lovely. Even when she was all covered in mud she was lovely. We love her—and you sent her away without seeing me…'

'I didn't send her away…'

'Yes, you *did*.' Katie's voice rose in frustration. Tears welled in her eyes and started to fall. 'Yes, you did,' she repeated. 'Because Beth wouldn't go away unless you sent her. Not without seeing me. I know that. I know that about Beth

because…because she loves us. I *know* she does. And if you
don't know that then…then you're stupid!'

It was too much for the little girl. Katie's voice broke on a
sob, and she threw Kell one last glare before she turned and
fled.

And Kell was left standing alone, staring after her, with the
child's words echoing round and round in his head.

'Beth wouldn't go away unless you sent her.'

Dear God…

It was the absolute truth. Kell knew that, as he had always
known the truth about Joanne. He'd known always that Joanne
would leave.

As he knew Beth would stay.

'If you don't know that then you're stupid…'

You do know that, Kell Hallam, he told himself savagely.
You know she loves us. But you've sent her away. You stupid,
stupid fool, you've sent her away. You've made her cry and
you've made her leave you.

So bring her back. Dear God, follow her. Bring her back.
Love her…

Kell took a step towards the door, but as he did the telephone started to ring.

Beth shoved her foot hard on the accelerator as soon as she
turned out of Kell Hallam's gate, wanting to put distance between herself and heartbreak as fast as possible—but the pain
couldn't be eased with distance.

Her car found the way back to her farm all by itself. It must
have done so—because Beth surely didn't drive it. Afterwards
she could hardly remember the drive home. That she didn't
hit anything was a miracle in itself.

What now? What now? her heart kept demanding, and there
was no answer at all.

There was an answer of sorts when she arrived at the farm.

Lyle was waiting. One erstwhile bridegroom had come to claim his own.

Beth's cousin seemed to have been waiting for a while. There was no sign of his presence as Beth drove in—obviously he'd parked his car out of sight—but as she entered the back door she found Lyle, seated at her kitchen table with a plate of eggs on toast before him.

Lyle...

There were so many things Beth wanted to say to her cousin. So much anger... Instead, Beth's mind was numb with misery—and all she could think of was that Lyle was eating her food.

Lyle was eating *her* eggs, Beth saw, her mind reacting to what should have been the least of her annoyances with irrational anger. *Her eggs!* After what this man had tried to do to Katie... That he could sit here eating her eggs—eggs collected by Katie and cooked with firewood from the tree Kell had helped her fell...

The heartbreak of the past few hours was all around her, and Beth felt her emotions shift again, venting themselves in almost mindless fury. This was all Lyle's fault, she thought illogically. All of it!

It was all she could do not to stride across and dump the plate of food in her cousin's immaculately suited lap. Instead she forced herself to stand still in the doorway and make her voice icily calm.

'You...'

'Beth.' Lyle pushed his plate of food away in distaste and rose to face her. 'It's about time you arrived. Where the hell have you been?'

'It's none of your business, Lyle.'

'No?'

And then suddenly Beth's anger gave way to fear. Lyle

Mayberry was pudgy and balding and not too tall—but the look in his eyes as he faced her now was not the look of a benign cousin. The look was one of pure malevolence.

Beth had seen that look before—had told herself that her cousin must have grown out of his awful childhood mood swings—but now she wasn't the least bit sure that he had.

'It is my business, Beth,' Lyle told her, his voice smooth as silk. He walked over to her, reached behind and shut the door. Closing out the outside world... 'You jilted me. Because of you I stand to lose two million dollars.'

'The money's not yours, Lyle.' Beth edged away, her eyes not leaving his face. 'I don't know what tricks you used to make the old man sign away his fortune—'

'What tricks I used are none of your business,' Lyle snapped. 'As if it's anything to you. The old man had no one else to leave things to.'

'Except his employees, who'd been faithful to him for a lifetime.' It was so hard to make her voice work. So hard to concentrate on what Lyle had done when all Beth wanted to do was weep for a love that wasn't wanted. But she had to make herself say it. 'And one granddaughter,' she whispered. 'A child who needs an inheritance so badly...'

'That damned kid should have died in an orphanage overseas,' Lyle threw at her. 'If I'd had any sense I would have hired someone to finish her off where it was relatively easy. I didn't realise the kid had an uncle...'

The fear welling in Beth was tightening to a cold knot. She was starting to feel cold through and through. Hire someone to kill Katie? Dear heaven, if he'd do that...what else was he capable of? 'Maybe you should have found that out before you made your plans,' she told him. 'Found out that Katie has someone who loves her.'

'Loves her!' Lyle snapped. 'A bloody half-brother of her

mother who thinks he can control the kid and get the money for himself?'

'Kell wouldn't…'

Lyle wasn't listening. 'How much is Hallam paying you?' he demanded.

'Nothing.'

'Liar. I read your note.'

'I didn't write the note, Lyle,' Beth said tiredly. 'Kell posed as a photographer and abducted me on the day of the wedding. He wrote the note. You see…? It's possible for someone else to be as ruthless as you.'

'He abducted you?' Lyle stood back on his heels and stared at Beth in disbelief. 'I don't believe it.'

'It's the truth.'

Silence.

'Well, if it's true…' Lyle's eyes became calculating. 'There's three more days until my birthday and the marriage licence is still good. My offer still stands, Beth.'

'Thirty thousand dollars to marry you?' Beth fought down rising hysteria. Offers from all sides. And some worse than others. She shook her head. 'Lyle, you told me no one would be hurt—but one little girl stands to lose her entire family background if you inherit. Everything she's ever cared about. I'm sorry, but if the choice of inheritance is between you and Katie, then the choice has to be Katie.'

'You slut!' And before Beth could recoil Lyle hit her, slapping her hard across the face.

Lyle had hit Beth before. Many times. It came as no shock. She simply closed her eyes, took a step back and waited. She'd learned in the past that to react with fear would only make him worse.

'There's nothing you can do, Lyle,' Beth said gently, resisting the urge to put up a defensive hand to her bruised face. 'You lied to me and you were found out. I'm not marrying

you and that's an end to it. You can be as angry as you wish—
but it won't make any difference.'

Silence.

And when Beth opened her eyes Lyle wasn't wearing his
look of baffled fury. There was a gleam of malicious triumph
in his eyes.

The old fear settled back—and stayed.

'That's not an end of it,' Lyle said silkily. 'You think I
haven't been busy these last ten days? I didn't have a honeymoon to go on, so I thought I'd spend the time thinking
about you instead. About how stupid you made me feel. About
losing two million dollars. And about how you can be forced
to marry me and live to regret you made me look a fool.'

'I can't be forced.'

'I think you can.' And Lyle drew out a sheaf of papers and
laid them on the table. 'See these?' He smiled. 'These are our
marriage contracts. The marriage takes place officially tomorrow—two days before my birthday—but according to these
documents it's already taken place and been witnessed.
There'll be a notice in Saturday's newspapers explaining our
wedding took place privately.'

He smiled. 'I've spread it round that you're a country girl
at heart and the thought of such a big wedding scared you.
That's why you ran. But deep down you really love me,
Beth—so, of course, you've married me privately now. Our
marriage was made in heaven, my love.' He smirked. 'Let no
man put us asunder—especially Kelsey Hallam.'

'You're mad,' Beth whispered. 'Mad.'

'Not mad.' Lyle smirked again. 'Just very, very careful this
time, Bethany. Last time I left it to you to get to the church—
but I'm taking no chances now. Our marriage celebrant has
been paid handsomely not only to provide me with these documents but also to keep himself right out sight tomorrow—so
no one can say the wedding didn't take place. Likewise the

two witnesses. They'll swear black and blue they attended
Roger Scanley's offices and witnessed the ceremony. The documents only need your signature and the whole thing's fool-
proof.'

'As if I would…'

'Oh, I think you will,' Lyle said smoothly. 'As soon as
you've seen these.' And he flipped a handful of pictures from
his top pocket and tossed them onto the table.

Beth didn't want to pick them up. She didn't want to give
him that pleasure. She stared at her horrible cousin for a long
moment, and the smirk on his face grew broader.

'You don't really have a choice, cousin,' he said softly. 'It's
what you might call a matter of life and death. Look at the
pictures.'

And finally Beth lifted the photographs.

Georgie.

Here were photographs of her young cousin, Georgie
Gallagher. Fourteen years old, gangly, full of fun—and one of
the few people in the world Beth had loved for years. Beth
flicked them over, feeling more and more fearful as she did.
The photographs had clearly been taken without Georgie seeing, and they were of the girl at home. Watching television.
Talking to her mother in the kitchen. Sleeping…

'This is Peeping Tom stuff,' she said. 'Why have you
taken…?'

'Keep going.'

Beth flicked the pictures over, her heart growing colder at
each shot.

The next picture was of an electricity fuse box—a full view
showing it against the wall of Georgie's bedroom and then a
closer shot.

And then a closer one still, showing a small attachment at
the base of the box.

'What…what have you done?' she managed.

'I haven't done a thing yet,' Lyle told her blandly. 'Unless you mean helping Oliver Bromley's death along by a few changes to his medication. I *did* do that—not that it's able to be proved. But as for Georgie... I haven't touched her. Not yet. But...'

'But what?'

'What you see there, Bethany, is a small electronic device capable of remote control detonation. Detonation, cousin. I suppose you know what that means?'

'You...' Beth's face drained of colour and her legs seemed to sag under her.

'I can see you understand, my clever bride.' Lyle tittered. 'You're right, of course. A nice little bomb. Tiny, but it's actually amazingly powerful. At first blast the fuse box will be fully alight. You remember the lay-out of our little cousin's room? The fuse box is on the outer wall, right between window and door. The blast will mean our precious cousin won't be able to escape. And the pure joy of doing it this way—as I told you, I really have been busy over the last ten days and I've learned such a lot—is that after such a fierce fire the investigators won't be able to tell more than it started in a fuse box.

'Old wiring, cousin. Tragic accident. Maybe we'd even have to cut short our honeymoon to attend the funeral. Because you still would marry me, Beth dear. You might just have to be a bit more hurt—if Georgie was already dead.'

'You'd do that?' Beth's heart froze in horror. 'You'd do that to Georgie?'

'I'll do anything for two million dollars,' Lyle said grimly. 'I checked you were back here before making all these arrangements. The reason I dated the wedding tomorrow was to make sure everything was ready and I could find you. It did give me a bad start when you took yourself off yesterday—

really, I had quite a bad time waiting this morning—but then you returned, like the dear, sweet bride you are.

'So, Beth... all you have to do is sign—and I wouldn't waste time if I were you. It's such a small electronic remote control device—and I have such an itchy finger.'

Beth stared in horror at her cousin. He looked as he always did when he made some helpless creature suffer. He looked as if he was enjoying every minute of it, and Beth knew he was.

'Georgie's in bed by ten at night,' he said smoothly. 'She's safe enough until then. But I really would like to try out my little device, Beth. You know that. So sign, there's a good girl.'

'If I sign, will you destroy the detonator?'

'No.' He shook his head. 'You think I'm a fool? Sign, destroy my leverage and have you racing off crying that our marriage was a farce? Even if I consummate our marriage— which, by the way, I'm quite looking forward to—my lawyer says we need to be seen as happily content after I turn thirty. You'll do my bidding until the world has seen you as my bride—until after my birthdate.'

And what then?

Beth's lips formed the question but the sound didn't come out. Dear heaven... Beth looked at her cousin and knew without being told just what he intended. There was too much enjoyment here to be explained simply by forcing Beth to sign a marriage contract against her will.

What would happen if Beth signed her marriage documents, was seen as married for a few days and then was released to tell the world her story? If Beth could prove Lyle had forced her to marry him, then their marriage contract would be annulled, and Lyle still wouldn't gain his inheritance. As well as that... Lyle had now boasted to Beth that he'd assisted in

Oliver Bromley's death. Could he afford to do that if he thought…if he thought she could tell others?

Dear heaven…

'What do you intend to do with me…until after your birthday?' she asked softly, and Lyle's smile widened.

'Why, go on a honeymoon, of course,' he told her. 'All the best couples do. Tomorrow we'll be seen dining tête-à-tête in an exclusive Sydney restaurant—and then we'll fly up north to board a yacht. We'll sail the Whitsundays. It's idyllic at this time of the year.'

'You hate sailing,' Beth said flatly—and shivered.

'Needs must,' Lyle told her gently, and smiled. And then Beth knew what her fate would be. Tragic honeymoon drowning… She could see it in the way he looked at her.

'Sign the papers, Beth,' Lyle hissed, pushing the documents before her. 'And don't do anything foolish. I have duplicates in case you smudge your signature, but any more than one accident and my finger would get itchy. Sign. Now.' And he raised his hand to hit her again.

The world stood still.

And then suddenly it started revolving again—revolving till Beth felt she would surely fall. There were people bursting through the door…and shouting…and one voice raised above all the rest.

'Touch her and I'll throttle you. Don't sign anything, Beth. Leave her alone, you—'

And Beth spun round—to find Kell moving through the door and across the room, shoving Lyle aside as if he was nothing as he moved to take her into his arms.

It wasn't just Kell. Behind and around Kell there were police officers, and more behind them. Almost before Kell had spoken they'd reached Beth's cousin, were seizing Lyle's arms, twisting them up behind him and searching him for weapons in what seemed one seamless action.

And in seconds there was a tiny electronic device—similar to a television remote control only in miniature—lying on the table. Also one wickedly evil-looking gun.

Beth was so dazed she could have fallen, but there was no chance of that. She was wrapped tight in the arms of her beloved Kell—and she was being held as if she would never be released.

She was being held as if she were more precious than life itself.

CHAPTER TWELVE

IT TOOK a long time for explanations to come.

There seemed so much to do. The policemen filled the room, four in all, and overpowering in their presence, and Lyle seemed to shrink inside his suit while Beth watched.

Beth stayed absolutely motionless in Kell's hold while the policemens' questions barked out. The questioning was hard and fast, but Lyle stayed obstinately silent. Then one of the police officers produced a tape recorder and replayed the conversation that had just occurred between Beth and Lyle, while another continued to snap questions at Lyle—and as the tape played on all the colour and bluster faded from Lyle's face.

And all the time Kell held Beth with infinite tenderness, his face in her hair and his heart against hers. He was listening to what was happening but only with half an ear. His attention was almost totally focused on the girl in his arms.

The tape went on and on. The police had recorded every word Lyle had spoken to Beth—and at the end of the tape Lyle looked as if he no longer fitted his suit. He looked shrunken and pallid and sick.

But from where Beth stood she didn't feel sorry for him at all. Not one bit. She stood in the safety of Kell's arms, with her face against the coarseness of his shirt, and she felt her body tremble from head to foot with the horror of what Lyle had said to her. What he said that he'd done—and what he'd threatened.

Beth had known Lyle was evil. But that he could be *so* evil? To kill…?

Kell held her hard, as if he knew that only his body was

between Beth and absolute horror. If he released her then she couldn't bear it. Beth shivered uncontrollably in the warmth of the summer's afternoon and Kell swore softly against her hair.

'Don't fear, love,' he whispered. 'Don't. It's over. Over. He'll never come near you again—I swear. Dear God, I swear.'

And then the policemen were finally finished. Lyle was ushered outside, sagging between two police officers. A senior sergeant was talking to Kell and Beth, and Kell was turning her to listen.

'We'll need to get your statements, miss,' the policeman said, with an apologetic look at Kell. Then, after another look and unspoken message, the policeman nodded in decision. 'But it can wait until tomorrow. If you could bring Miss Lister into the local police station tomorrow, sir?'

'I'll do that,' Kell told him, his arms around Beth tightening further. 'Do you have enough evidence to charge him?'

'Oh, we have enough.' There was grim satisfaction in the policeman's voice. 'We're grateful for the tip-off, sir.' Then, at Beth's look of confusion, he went further. 'We've had Mr Mayberry under our eye for a while,' he told Beth. 'There were a few unexplained facts around Oliver Bromley's death that had us worried.

'At the time, Bromley's death seemed to have been caused by an accidental mix-up of medicines, but the dismissal of all near employees just before Bromley died made us wonder. Still, there was nothing we could prove. Now, though...as well as a cast-iron case of inheritance fraud, we have a nice little admission which may mean we can bring a case of murder against him.'

He smiled. 'It's a bonus, if I do say so,' he told them, his satisfaction obvious. 'After your phone call, Mr Hallam, we came to check on Miss Lister, and after some thought we left the police vehicle concealed beyond the boundaries. We knew we had a bit of time before Miss Lister arrived—though she came faster than you'd said she would, sir.

'When we saw how overgrown the back of the house was, and how close we could get to the open windows at the back without Mayberry seeing us, we figured a tape of any conversation might just be profitable. So…we organised the tape just before Miss Lister arrived, and it's certainly given us value for our efforts.' One more broad grin at both of them. 'Now—if I can leave Miss Lister to your care, sir—we'll be off. Can I do that?'

Kell looked down at Beth, and in his look was an expression that she hardly knew. An expression she could hardly hope she was seeing.

'Yes, Sergeant, I'll take care of Miss Lister,' Kell said softly, and he now had eyes only for Beth. 'I'll take care of Bethany. For just as long as she'll have me.'

And neither of them saw the policeman take his leave.

They only saw each other.

It was a good ten minutes before Kell released Bethany by as much as an inch, and by the time he did a lot of her questions had already been answered.

The questions of her heart…

Kell was holding her in his arms as if he'd never let her go. His hands—his eyes—his body—all declared it without a word being uttered. Something had changed. Something had moved within Kell to make him love Beth as she loved in return. And despite the horror of the afternoon—despite Beth's fear—all she felt now was joy. Sheer, piercing joy in every inch of her body.

But there were things she still didn't understand. Mundane…but necessary to know. To explain the joy.

'Kell…' Somehow Beth made her hands push him back— just a further inch or so—certainly not far enough to escape the feel of his arms around her. 'Kell, I don't understand. This morning you acted as if you hated me.' She shook her head at him and managed a shy smile. 'Would you mind telling me just what the heck is going on?'

'I thought you'd guessed.' Kell smiled back down at her and his hand came up to touch the bruise on her cheek. 'He hit you, Beth. The murdering b—'

'Hush.' Beth's hand came up to seize Kell's fingers and hold them. 'I won't think of him. Not now.'

'If I'd come a minute earlier I would have stopped him before he did this. The police wanted that tape too much. They said he hit you before they realised he intended it, that when he tried again they moved, but they should have stopped him sooner...'

'You weren't there?' Beth whispered. 'I thought with the tape...you must have been outside all the time.'

'Not me,' Kell said grimly, pulling her in to lie against him. 'I was driving faster than I've ever driven in my life, and I reached here just as the police burst in. I'm sure if I'd been here earlier I'd never have let him go so far. That he hit you...'

He put a hand up to run his fingers through her hair. 'Beth, I've never been more frightened in my life as I was driving here. And the overpowering fear... I kept thinking, if Mayberry hurt you then you'd be hurt by both of us. I'd hurt you so much this morning. I'd tried to drive you away and I was so damned cruel. So cruel...'

'Don't.'

'It's true,' Kell whispered into her hair. 'And your accusations were true. I was so afraid to love. Laura... Beth, my little Laura was only three years old when she died, and I decided then that nothing—no one—was going to touch me emotionally for the rest of my life. I'd never allow myself to feel pain like that. Only Katie needed me so much...

'And then there was you, sweet Beth, offering me your love no matter how cruel I'd been to you. And finally I got the phone call telling me where Mayberry was, and I knew then that any decision I'd made in the past was well and truly useless. I've never…' Kell hesitated. He pulled Beth tighter and a shudder ran through his long body. 'I've never known such fear.'

'Kell…I don't understand.'

'I've had a private detective keeping tabs on Mayberry,' Kell told her. 'Insurance, if you like. I just wanted to know where he was all the time up until his birthday. There were a few worrying things—a visit to a marriage celebrant with a dubious reputation. Not enough to really worry me, though. And the detective thought his visits to your little cousin's house innocuous enough—after all, they were relatives, and my detective didn't know how close. He seemed to have a key.'

'He was planting…'

'I know that now,' Kell said grimly. 'But after he'd gone through the high front gate of Georgie's house, my detective had no way of knowing what was happening. After his visit to the marriage celebrant I thought he might be trying to marry someone else without a licence, but I thought we could always overturn that. Then my detective lost him—but a few minutes after you left today he telephoned to say not to worry—Mayberry had gone to ground in a remote little farmhouse. He'd been there all night and was still there. This farm house. And I knew…*then* I knew… That you were in danger.'

'So you came…'

'I was about to come anyway,' Kell said bleakly. 'After you'd gone, Katie saw you go and came to me, demanding to know why you hadn't visited her. Then she said that you loved us and that I was stupid. And I sat there, remembering the dreadful look on your face as you'd left—as if I'd struck you harder than Mayberry has—and it dawned on me that Katie was absolutely right. That I'd been comparing you to Joanne and to do such a thing was just plain crazy. And then the detective rang and I knew I'd put you in danger. In deadly danger.'

'Kell…'

'I had to waste time phoning the police then,' Kell told her bleakly, and the remembrance of fear was in his voice. 'I thought your car was slow, so I'd have time… Dear heaven, you must have driven your car into the ground to get here before me. But at least the police were here.

'I told them I suspected Mayberry would try to force you to marry him, and asked could they send local men to ensure your safety. Only then I was put through to a senior officer in the homicide division. It seemed the police already had their suspicions about Mayberry. They said they'd come—but that they'd try to set up a surveillance team rather than arrest him on the spot. You see, unless he was actually recorded making threats there would be nothing we could touch him with.'

'So that's why…'

'That's why the police were here without either you or Mayberry knowing,' Kell said grimly. 'And then I put the phone down and I started to imagine what would happen if you refused to marry Mayberry. I knew because of Katie that you would refuse. I started to be so afraid that something would happen…that the police wouldn't move in time…'

His arms held her and a shudder racked his long frame. 'Dear God, Beth, my drive here seemed the longest drive in history. If anything had happened to you… You've given me such a gift…and I threw it back at you. You've given me your love…' He shuddered again, and then pushed her away to arm's length so he could see her face.

'Beth, I don't deserve you,' he murmured softly. 'I don't deserve anyone as beautiful—as loving—as big-hearted as my lovely Beth. I've treated you abominably—and yet… Beth, will you forgive me? Will you keep loving me? Because if I've lost your love—'

'No!' Beth stood on tiptoes to lightly kiss his lips. Her eyes were bright with unshed tears. 'Kell, how can I stop loving you? Loving you is just something that I do. It's like breathing. It's as much a part of me as that. You are a part of me, Kell Hallam, and you are that whatever you do. Wherever you go. You are my love.'

For a long moment Kell stood looking down into Beth's eyes—and what he saw there made the tension slowly ebb right out of him. He exhaled in one long sigh, and then he pulled her into him again.

'Darling Beth,' he whispered. 'My own sweet love. Will you help me learn to love again? Beth, you asked me to love you. If you'll let me, then I intend to start right now and make up for lost time—and I don't intend to stop until we reach ninety-nine or older. And then I'll write passionate letters from the far end of the nursing home, sweet Beth. But for now…'

For now…

For now there was no doubt what he intended. Kell's lips met hers, and their kiss grew deeper and deeper, and somewhere inside each of them a need arose that would not be sated by mere kissing. A need that had them clinging to each other in an ecstasy of passion that could have only one end. Or maybe only one beginning.

But there was something…*someone* who must be remembered.

'But…what about Katie?' Beth's voice was barely above a whisper, and it was all she could do to frame the words. She wanted this man so badly. Her man. Her life. 'Is Katie home by herself? Kell…'

'Katie is not home by herself,' Kell told her, lifting his lips a whole quarter of an inch back from hers to let her speak.

Then, as if he couldn't bear to be so far away, he lifted her to lie in his arms—a willing, loving captive. 'Katie is with my housekeeper and my farm manager and my sundry employees—all of whom have promised to take the utmost care of her.'

'But she'll be unhappy. Kell, you mustn't stay here. You must go…'

'I must *not* go.' Kell was striding towards the bedroom now, and his eyes were alight with love and laughter. 'Before I left I made Katie a promise. "I'm off to find our Bethany," I told her. "And I'll bring her home as my bride." I made our Katie a promise, my Beth. Would you have me break it? Will you be my bride, my darling Beth? Forever and forever and forever?'

And Beth twined her arms around her lover's body and welcomed her Kell into her heart—there was no need for an answer.

There was no need for words, now and for ever.

'Wow, Beth! You look fabulous!'

Bethany Lister turned to her young cousin and grinned.

'That's what you said last time, Georgie Gallagher, when I was all dolled up in satin and lace. What's a girl to believe?'

Georgie gave a rueful chuckle and surveyed Beth with affection.

'Yeah, well, last time it was a gorgeous dress,' she admitted. 'But this time it's you.' She moved across to lift Beth's curls and ruffle them so they floated free around Beth's shoulders. 'It's the Beth I love.'

The dress was simplicity itself. Georgie had helped Beth choose it, and the first time they'd seen it they'd known it was right. It was of fine Swiss cotton, with tiny sleeves just covering Beth's shoulders, the fabric clinging gently to Beth's breasts and then floating free in lovely soft folds to her feet.

She wore no veil and no other adornment. The dress was white and plain and very, very lovely.

'And there's no room for a possum in this one.' Georgie chuckled. 'Not that you need to hide anything here.'

There certainly wasn't. Beth looked out of the windows of Kell's home, down to where the wedding guests were gathered. Not so many this time, but so much more welcome. All the people she loved, Kell loved, Katie loved.

Plus the odd animal. Edna and Fred Walter had conjured up a few of Beth's old patients to join the ceremony—those animals who'd been too badly damaged to be rehabilitated and had become pets over the years.

For heaven's sake, from here Beth could see two wallabies, one fat wombat and there was a great white cockatoo, sitting on Fred Walter's shoulders and giving cheek to Kell's two dogs. As Beth watched, the bird launched itself off to fly to a new perch—high on Madge Trotter's hat. The ensuing squawk from the hotel-keeper had everyone laughing, and the dogs' barking became almost hysterical. This was some crazy wedding party!

It was the wedding party Beth wanted, and they were all where she wanted them to be. Where she wanted to be married. They were all on the bridge—Kell's wonderful wooden bridge over his river, the place Beth remembered looking up to him and falling so deeply in love. They'd set it up to look almost like a chapel—with huge boughs of mistletoe hanging overhead to form a canopy through which the sun glinted like rays of light through a stained glass window.

Mistletoe... 'coolbunna' meant mistletoe, Beth thought mistily, and Coolbunna was her home. Beth's home and Kell's home and Katie's home, and they'd be surrounded by mistletoe for the rest of their lives.

'We're ready. Uncle Kell's ready and he's waiting.' It was a whoop of excitement from outside, and in rushed Katie. The child was resplendent in pink flounces—'Because pink really is my favourite'—and in her arms she carried a big rag doll, ceremoniously dressed in Katie's old blue pinafore. Both doll and Katie wore sheaves of pink ribbon. They looked amazing—and Katie's expression said she thought they both looked splendid.

'Oh, Beth,' Katie squeaked. 'You're almost as pretty as Madeleine and me.' She took a deep breath, vanity and generosity at war. She really was a nice child, though.

'You can…' She gulped. 'You can wear my pink ribbons if you like, Beth,' she offered.

And Beth scooped her up and gave her a fast, hard hug.

'Katie-bell, that is quite the best offer that's ever been made to me.' Beth's eyes pricked with tears of pride and she set the little one on her feet again. 'But Georgie, here, says my hair needs to be free.'

'It does, too,' Georgie declared. 'It's what Beth is, Katie-bell. A free spirit. Don't you agree?'

Katie looked up in confusion. 'Free…' She frowned. 'Does that mean me and Uncle Kell will have to let her go?'

And Beth laughed, took the small child's hand and walked outside to where her wedding guests were waiting.

To where Kell was waiting.

He was there, standing waiting under the mistletoe, his face as proud and as happy as a man's could be. In his deep black suit he looked so magnificent that Beth almost gasped aloud. Her Kell…

And Kell thought the same. As Beth appeared, he closed his eyes for one brief instant, and when he opened them the look in his eyes told her all she would ever want to know.

'No, Katie, it doesn't mean you and Kell will ever need to let me go,' Beth whispered, taking Kell's hand in hers and looking up at him with eyes that returned his love a hundredfold. 'Because, like all free creatures who know their own heart, this one knows where home is. Home is where the heart is, Katie-bell. And home is here.'

LOOK FOR OUR FOUR FABULOUS MEN!

Each month some of today's bestselling authors bring
four new fabulous men to Harlequin American Romance.
Whether they're rebel ranchers, millionaire power brokers
or sexy single dads, they're all gallant princes—and
they're all ready to sweep you into lighthearted fantasies
and contemporary fairy tales where anything is possible
and where all your dreams come true!

You don't even have to make a wish...
Harlequin American Romance will grant your every desire!

Look for Harlequin American Romance
wherever Harlequin books are sold!

HARLEQUIN PRESENTS®

HARLEQUIN PRESENTS
men you won't be able to resist
falling in love with...

HARLEQUIN PRESENTS
women who have feelings
just like your own...

HARLEQUIN PRESENTS
powerful passion in
exotic international settings...

HARLEQUIN PRESENTS
intense, dramatic stories that will keep you
turning to the very last page...

HARLEQUIN PRESENTS
The world's bestselling romance series!

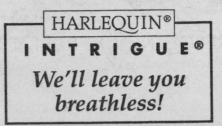

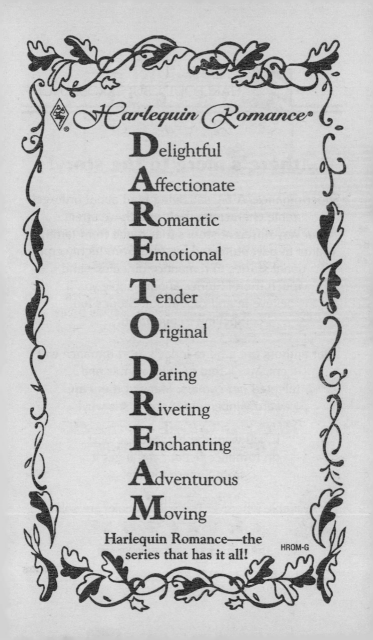

Harlequin Romance®

Delightful

Affectionate

Romantic

Emotional

Tender

Original

Daring

Riveting

Enchanting

Adventurous

Moving

Harlequin Romance—the
series that has it all!

HROM-G

HARLEQUIN SUPERROMANCE®

...there's more to the story!

Superromance. A *big* satisfying read about unforget-
table characters. Each month we offer
four very different stories that range from family
drama to adventure and mystery, from highly emotional stories to romantic comedies—and
much more! Stories about people you'll
believe in and care about. Stories too
compelling to put down....

Our authors are among today's *best* romance writ-
ers. You'll find familiar names and
talented newcomers. Many of them are
award winners—and you'll see why!

If you want the biggest and best
in romance fiction, you'll get it
from Superromance!

Available wherever Harlequin books are sold.